WITHDRAWN

WHAT REMAINS

HELENE DUNBAR

D0096798

flux®

Woodbury, Minnesota

First Edition
First Printing, 2015

Book design by Bob Gaul
Cover design by Ellen Lawson
Cover images: iStockphoto.com/10064547/©mattjeacock
iStockphoto.com/34261462/©VeselovaElena
iStockphoto.com/43072668/©Balkonsky

Flux, an imprint of Llewellyn Worldwide Ltd.

Library of Congress Cataloging-in-Publication Data
Dunbar, Helene.
   What remains/Helene Dunbar.—First edition.
      pages cm
   Summary: After surviving a car crash that kills his best friend Lizzie, sixteen-year-old Cal Ryan must work through his grief and figure out his relationship with their other best friend, Spencer.
   ISBN 978-0-7387-4430-8
   [1. Best friends—Fiction. 2. Friendship—Fiction. 3. Death—Fiction. 4. Grief—Fiction.] I. Title.
   PZ7.D79428Wh 2015
   [Fic]—dc23

                                                  2014048471

                              Flux
                    Llewellyn Worldwide Ltd.
                      2143 Wooddale Drive
                    Woodbury, MN 55125-2989
                        www.fluxnow.com

              Printed in the United States of America

To:
Tami Davis Brenner, Laurin Buchanan, Lindsay Craig,
Suzanne Kamata, Patrick Northway, Ike Pulver,
Emilie Richmond, Scott Sitner, Tom Tanner,
and Christopher Tower

Lux Esto

And to John, because in a way they're all for you.

ONE

No one ever calls in the middle of the night to tell you that you've won the lottery.

Or that you aced your chem final.

Or that your favorite team won the series.

If the phone rings in the middle of the night, it's a pretty sure bet someone has died. Or broken up with his girlfriend. Or, in my case, that something awful has happened to Lizzie.

She doesn't always call me. Sometimes she calls Spencer. Sometimes, I suspect, she just deals with her mom's drinking and her loser stepfather's temper and doesn't tell either of us. I hate that even more than I hate the phone ringing in the middle of the night.

This time when it rings, I'm dreaming that I'm kissing Ally Martin while standing on first base on Maple Grove's baseball field. Yeah, I'm getting to first base on first base. My subconscious obviously has a sense of humor.

I know I'm dreaming because you can't really kiss someone you haven't had the courage to speak to. But that doesn't keep me from pulling her closer and, as I do, her breasts rub against me and suddenly I know why most guys have been drooling over girls while I've been perfecting my swing and kicking myself for being too much of a coward to even talk to her.

My cell keeps ringing, shrill and demanding. I pull

my hand away from Ally and fumble around on my night-stand just as the Maple Grove Mustangs' theme song stops.

Somehow, I resist the urge to smash the phone against the wall in frustration. Then it starts again and I take a deep breath because it doesn't seem like I've done that in a while. On the screen I see two things at the same time. It's two in the morning. And it's Lizzie calling.

My voice cracks a little when I answer. I really just want to be back in that place in my head where baseball and Ally converge.

"Cal, I need you to come get me." Lizzie's voice is rushed and insistent enough to pull me out of bed.

It's been a long time since she needed me to get her in the middle of the night. Whatever lingering hope I had about returning to my dream disappears and she has all my attention.

Still, I have to blink a few times to make sure I'm really awake. "Where are you? Are you okay?"

On the other end of the phone, glasses clink, traffic hums, and raised voices are, well, raised. It's a combination of sounds that make my teeth ache.

Lizzie answers, "I'm outside Sidewinders. You know, at fourth and Madison?"

My stomach drops and the muscles in my neck tighten like I've taken a bad swing at an outside pitch. It's a school night and I can't think of any good reason for her to be outside a bar at the edge of a crappy part of Detroit.

"What the hell are you doing there?" I ask, although I'm not totally sure I want to hear her answer.

"Can we save story time for later? I'll explain everything but I need you to come get me." She sounds impatient even though she knows there's no chance I won't come for her. I always come when Lizzie calls.

"Yeah, be there in five." I hang up without wasting the time to say goodbye. It's usually a ten-minute drive. It won't be tonight.

I pull on yesterday's jeans, grab a T-shirt off the floor, and throw on some sneakers without bothering to tie them. I'm sure my hair is all sorts of crazy, but it isn't like that with me and Lizzie. It isn't like that with me and anybody except in my dreams. Besides, I'm unlikely to run into anyone I know near Sidewinders.

I've learned the hard way that I'm not going to make it out the front door without waking my parents and that's a conversation I'm not eager to have more than once in a lifetime, so I slink through the kitchen to the back door and out around the side of the house.

My Corolla is in its usual space a few houses away in preparation for occasions like this, but it feels farther. The sky is the kind of dark it gets when it isn't really night anymore, but it isn't morning either. The street is creepy quiet, which makes every other sound way too loud: my steps on the concrete; the sound of the car door opening and then closing; a raccoon rummaging in a garbage can. It's the kind of quiet that things hide in.

I crank up the stereo, hoping to force the silence out of the car. Two guys on talk radio are debating whether or not the American League should do away with the designated hitter rule. Usually I'd care, but tonight I can't work up an opinion.

I kill the volume and drive, not even looking at the speedometer. I can't figure out what might have happened to make Lizzie call *this time*. All I can come up with is that, since Spencer and I bought her a phone to use when things are bad, I guess they are.

My tires squeal around the corner at Fourth. Lizzie is standing in front of the bar in a slightly paint-stained black dress with her long, dark hair pinned back, one purple-dyed strand hanging down free from the clip. I idle at the curb and lean over to hug her as she gets in. "Are you okay? Should I take you home?" I don't bother to mention that she hasn't buckled her seat belt. It doesn't seem like the right time for that age-old fight.

"Not home," she says as she rolls her eyes and plants her worn Doc Martin wannabes on the dash.

I feel stupid. Of course she doesn't want to go home. Home is what caused this in the first place and I'm an idiot for even suggesting it.

"Just take me somewhere," she demands.

I nod and start to drive us back into a better neighborhood, which is pretty much any area other than this one. Soon we're in the parking lot near the playground of the old monastery. I have no idea why a monastery needs a playground. I mean, the monks don't have kids or anything, but it's always a good quiet place to come. It's late enough that even the stoners and the couples looking for a parent-free place to make out have gone home.

We don't say a word until we get out of the car and head over to the swings and then the not-knowing starts to get to me.

"Lizzie?"

We each grab a swing and I watch as she takes a deep breath.

"I was in the shed," she says. No surprise. Lizzie practically lives in the shed, which she's transformed into a make-shift art studio.

She pumps her legs so she's soaring, almost level with the top of the swing set, which is creaking from our weight. I don't try to match her altitude because I've got a thing about heights and I'm pretty sure my puking won't help anything.

I give Lizzie a few minutes to continue her story, but she doesn't say anything else. Her silence makes me more nervous than anything I'm expecting her to come out with and finally, I can't take it anymore. As she slows down, I get up and grab the chains of her swing to stop her.

"Come on, talk to me," I plead.

She looks up at me with tired, dark eyes and drags her boots in the dirt.

"I was working on a new piece when the old bat came home drunk and they started fighting," she says in a dull monotone. "I cranked my speakers, but I could still hear her screaming. I mean, if she was that loud I figured I needed to see what was up." Lizzie's eyes hold me in place, a challenge. Talking about this doesn't make her the least bit uncomfortable.

"What was it?" All of the tension in my voice makes up for the lack of any in hers.

"He hit her, I guess." She shrugs like it's no big deal that she had to listen to her mom getting smacked around. "When I went in, she was chasing him with that shitty orange lamp we have in the living room. I tried to stop her, but she started coming after me. I couldn't get her to back off so I just left."

I nod, wishing this sort of thing was rare at Lizzie's house but knowing it isn't.

I wait for the missing piece. "So how did you get to Sidewinders?" Lizzie can't afford a car and it's way too far for her to have walked.

Now she looks away because she already knows what my reaction is going to be and her voice is low when she answers. "Hitched. It's just where the guy on the bike was going."

I pause, trying to swallow the urge to yell at her. "Lizzie, you promised." I don't mean to give her a hard time, but she used to hitch a lot and it would literally keep me up at night, wondering if I was going to wake up to hear she'd been stabbed and dumped by the side of the road.

She scrunches up her face, knowing exactly how much her admission upsets me. "Yeah, sorry about that. I figured I'd just get away from them and then sort it out from there."

I'm suddenly aware that the chains of the swing are really, really cold. The frost covers the metal and bites at my freezing hands. I blow on them until they start to sting.

"You should have called me when you left the house," I tell her. "You didn't need to go out there."

"Yeah, I know." She twists her swing around and around

and then lets it unwind before she answers. "I guess I was hoping this wouldn't turn into one of those times where I needed a knight on a white horse to come rescue me."

I try to smile, but I'm pretty sure that I've only managed a twisted grimace. "I'm not much of a knight," I say, looking down at my rumpled jeans and untied shoes. "But you know I'm always here for you. Spencer and I both are."

She smirks. "Yeah, I think Spence might be fed up with my shit for a while."

"Why?" I ask, puzzled. "What is it?"

She doesn't answer right away. I put my hands, which are either numb or starting to get warm, I can't really tell, over hers.

Then she looks up at me, the streetlight reflected in her eyes. "I just get sick of it, you know. Being a pain in the ass. The two of you having to make sure poor Lizzie isn't in any trouble."

I kneel down in front of her so that we're eye-to-eye. "Is that really what you think? That we just love you out of pity or something?" I can hear the frustration in my words and am flooded with guilt. I'm determined not to be one more difficult thing in her life.

A lot of expressions cross her face and then it settles on one I really can't read. "We slept together, you know. Me and Spence."

I almost fall backwards. She isn't telling me this for shock value because *that* expression I know well. But whatever her intent, I *am* shocked. Really, really shocked. Like breath-catching-in-my-throat shocked. Not just shocked because Spencer is gay, though that's part of it. And not just because I didn't know, though that's part of it too. Really I'm shocked because ... I don't know. I just am. I mean, Lizzie has been totally in love with Spencer since the first time she met him, but Spencer ... well, that's more complicated.

But under the shock, I'm embarrassed because it confirms what I figured anyhow. I'm the only one of us that hasn't had sex. It shouldn't surprise me. It shouldn't really matter. But it does. It makes me feel like a total loser to have it confirmed just like that.

"I didn't," I say. "Know, I mean." I stand up and kick at the dirt under the swing, uncomfortable for too many reasons.

"Yeah. I can tell." She smiles and her face lights up. I'm not sure what's making her so happy; whether it's her memories, or that her secret was kept, or that she's pretty much rendered me speechless.

"And?" I'm not sure what I'm waiting for her to say. I certainly don't want a play-by-play. I guess I just want to know if this changes anything between all of us.

"There is no 'and.' It happened once. It was wonderful. It won't happen again and I can now cross having sex with Spencer Yeats off my bucket list. What more do I really have to live for?" She has that wry Lizzie look on her face now, the one where half her mouth is smiling and half is frowning. That's definitely an expression I know well and I don't want to go down the path she's dragging this conversation. As much as I don't want to know how wonderful sex with Spencer was, I equally don't want to hear about how she thinks she has nothing to live for.

8

I wrestle for something to make her feel better and settle on, "You know he loves you, right?"

"I know," she says softly and closes her eyes. "Just like he loves you."

I think of all the things the three of us have been through together since we met in first grade. "Is that really so bad?"

"No, of course not. I wouldn't trade it for anything," she admits. There's a small crack in her usual armor before she pulls it together and continues. "Well, except for the obvious. But I suppose being born the wrong sex to be with Spence is one more joke the universe has played on me."

"God, Lizzie…" My brain spins in the way it does when I see a hundred different options and all of them suck. Just like always, I'm helpless in the face of her hopelessness.

We've had assemblies at school on how to spot depression in our friends: loss of interest in doing things you like, sad thoughts, and on and on. But Lizzie hasn't lost interest or developed sad thoughts. She's always been this way.

Spencer knows how to deal with her when she's like this. He knows how to distract her and make her laugh. But I always feel like her sadness is stronger than me and drags me under so that I'm drowning with her instead of lifting us both up.

I lean over to hug her and we stay like that. Wrapped around each other. Quiet. Looking up at the stars. I point out that if she squints she can see the light of Saturn sitting just under the moon. I point out Polaris, the North Star, and tell her to wish on it, but she just smirks. Lizzie is convinced her wishes never come true.

So I try something else. "You know, Polaris won't even be the North Star forever. The way the Earth shifts means there have been other North Stars. Eventually when we look up in the sky it'll be another star we see there."

She looks at me, vaguely curious, but obviously unsure what I'm getting at. "Everything changes," I whisper into her hair, which smells a little like paint thinner. "It won't always be this hard."

Lizzie looks up at the sky and for a second I think maybe, just maybe, she gets it. Hope climbs up into my throat, but I choke on it when, in a voice filled with resignation, she says, "Yeah, but by then we'll all be dead."

Any dream I have of being able to make things better vanishes. I've failed her again and we both know it, so I stop trying. I just put my arms around her and hold on until we're both shivering and a sliver of sun appears over the horizon.

TWO

I drop Lizzie off and waited for her to flick on the porch light to tell me she's okay before I leave. Then I let the car idle through the still-too-quiet streets and try to ignore the churning of my stomach and the erratic beating of my heart.

I get home and into bed without bothering to take off my clothes. I have two hours to sleep before school, but instead of sleeping, I toss and turn and fixate on thoughts of Lizzie and Spencer having sex. Not thoughts of them actually *doing* anything ... just ... I feel like I should have known. That somehow, I'm a worse friend for not having noticed that something so significant had happened.

I get why Spencer didn't tell me. He'd think it was important to keep something like that private. But I have to wonder if Lizzie told me just to punish me for not paying attention or something. Maybe I've just been a shitty friend.

My guilt chases me all the way to my locker and right into Spencer who, as usual, is waiting for me, looking well-rested and relaxed. That changes when he sees me rumpled like I just rolled out of bed.

"What happened to you?" he asks.

My head feels like it's filled with cotton candy. I shake it before I mumble, "Lizzie."

"Crap. Is she okay? What was it this time?" Spencer is in total mother-hen mode now. More than I can handle at ten-to-eight a.m. He runs a hand through his dark curly hair and clenches his jaw, which makes his blue eyes look even more piercing than normal. It's a look he saves for crises involving me and Lizzie.

"She's fine." I don't say that I'm pretty sure she's in better shape than I am. "She's . . . " I'm lost for a word that works. "Lizzie."

Spencer scowls. He isn't going to let the issue go that easily and I'm too tired to put up a fight.

"Come on, Yeats." I sigh and smack his shoulder. "Let's go check on her and then you can relax."

I feel like I'm walking through fog as we make our way to her locker. Next to me, Spencer races down the hall like he's trying to put out a fire and despite my almost religious adherence to Coach's off-season training schedule, I'm hopeless at keeping up.

When we round the corner, Lizzie is already standing at her locker with a small container of paint in her hand. The end of a paint brush is stuck in her mouth as if she's puzzling over something.

Lizzie started painting the inside of her locker door the first week of freshman year. She did it when she was meant to be in class. She painted after school when Spencer and I were there for play rehearsal or baseball practice and snuck her in. And sometimes, like now, she does it before home room. I'm not really sure how she's managed never to get caught. Maybe the janitors are afraid of her or something.

From a distance, her locker door looks like a stained glass painting. The bottom shows the core of the earth and then the painting goes higher through ocean scenes, land and mountains, and finally into sky and space. I spent hours teaching her about constellations and planets so she'd get the top of it right and she nailed it. It's one of the most beautiful things I've ever seen, and the three of us have been talking about how we're going to take the door when we graduate next year.

Spencer is already standing behind her, admiring her work. I'm hoping he'll keep her distracted as I try to sneak up on her before she touches the brush to the inside of her locker.

But just as I'm getting close, she says, "Cal Ryan, if you mess this up, it's going to be the last thing you ever do."

I know she means it. No one screws with her art. So I drop my hands and try to pretend I hadn't been planning on scaring her.

"What are you adding now?"

She points to a tiny swing set in the corner of the painting with just a shadow of the monastery looming over it.

"You're a genius, you know," I say.

She smiles at us and dabs on more paint. "Of course. I've been telling you that for years."

Just then someone bumps into me hard, pushing me into Lizzie. Circles of black paint go flying all over her white skirt.

"Oops. Sorry," Justin Dillard says to a paint-stained Lizzie. He's our back-up varsity shortstop who doesn't get a ton of field time because that's my position and I'm rarely out of the game. "Guess you'll have to tell one of your boyfriends to clean that up. I bet it makes them hard when you order them around."

13

I can't keep my fists from clenching although I should be used to this shit by now. Ever since middle school there have been rumors about the three of us. Everyone would see me walking through the halls with my arm around Lizzie and then see her draped around Spencer at lunch. And Spencer and I were always hanging out. So of course in their minds there had to be more going on than us just being really close friends. The older we got, the more graphic and crazy the rumors became. They said that the three of us were hooking up. That we'd both gotten Lizzie pregnant. That Spencer and I were having some sort of wild S&M relationship. All of it was bullshit. We were just friends. Best friends.

Until now. Now that Spencer and Lizzie...

I need to talk to him about it, but at the moment all I can do is pull Lizzie behind me to try to keep her from doing something to make the situation worse. I don't even succeed at that. She flicks her brush. A wad of paint ends up on Dillard's cheek as she says, "Too bad you wouldn't know what being hard feels like, Your Impotence."

I pull myself up to my full height and expect Dillard to fight back, but he just gives me the finger and stalks off, wiping the paint from his face as he goes. Someday I'll figure out why there are never any teachers around when you need them.

Spencer is uncharacteristically quiet and on edge beside me, his arms wrapped tight against his chest. I can feel him breathing hard, but he's too smart to get into the fight he's itching for.

"If there's any such thing as karma, someone's going to hit a line drive straight into his balls," Lizzie says as she tries to clean the paint off her skirt with a cloth. Instead, though, all that's happening is that the paint is getting worked into the white fabric like crop circles.

"I've been working on my hit placement," I say, more serious than not. "I'll see what I can do."

"Do you want me to run you home at lunch to change clothes?" Spencer offers, ignoring our dreams of revenge. "I can ask to skip rehearsal."

"No, thanks. That's fine. I'll just...I don't know." Lizzie dips the cloth into the remaining paint and makes more circles around her skirt. When she's done it looks like the material might have come that way and she gives us a little smile.

I pull her into a quick hug, trying to avoid any paint that might still be wet. "That's one way to do it," I say as the first bell rings. "Hey, weren't you going to paint my locker at some point?"

"Yeah, I am. I just wanted to finish mine off first."

"You've been working on yours for almost three years, Liz," Spencer chimes in. "We're going to graduate before you get to Cal's."

"Well, then I'll have to make it something worth waiting for." Lizzie looks at her watch. "Shit. Gotta run," she says and bolts down the hall. She has art first period. It's the only class she cares about making it to on time.

The color slowly returns to Spencer's face as we watch her go.

"See, she's fine," I say. "Just like always."

"Yeah. Fine," he manages, unconvinced.

I just shake my head. Spencer doesn't get worked up by much, but he's always been overly protective of me and Lizzie. It makes me wonder what he was thinking when he decided to sleep with her. Did he feel guilty? Sorry for her? Was he even thinking that it might cause problems with the three of us by proving all of those stupid rumors true if anyone ever found out?

There isn't enough time before class to talk to him about it and I can't meet his eyes. "Later, Yeats."

The first bell rings and I'm almost relieved to rush off to English and slide into my seat.

Ben Evans, our catcher, sits next to me. He sticks his hand out for me to slap.

"Ready for the inaugural hour of lunch and laps?" he asks.

Crap. I knew I'd forgotten something. "Yeah, can't wait," I groan.

Coach Byrne's optional pre-season lunch-time practice isn't really optional and it doesn't involve lunch. It's all conditioning and strategy. I love the strategy parts. But I'd rather be out on the field throwing a ball around than running laps around a track.

"It'll all be worth it when we make it to the playoffs this year. And it's all on you, bro." Ben's optimism is catching. We came really close to taking it all last year. If I can keep my batting average up, he's probably right that we're on target to win it this year.

"No, no, there's no 'I' in team," I laugh, quoting one of the old posters that hang in the locker room. I'm not sure I agree with it, though. I mean, sure, it's all about sacrificing for the team, but you have to really want it for yourself too or you'll just sleepwalk through the games.

"Yeah," Ben replies. "But you're our secret weapon."

I try not to smile, but do anyhow. Baseball is one area of my life where I don't mind the pressure. It's almost like I become someone else once I step on the field, someone confident and brave.

I know I should say something self-deprecating, but I'm saved by the loudspeaker announcing that the lunchroom will be serving burgers today and there will be an assembly for juniors on how to study for the SATs during third period tomorrow.

As the voice drones on, I pull out a piece of paper.

I have this list. On the left side of the page sits all of the reasons why I should try to attract the attention of a pro scout. On the right side are all of the reasons why I should go to college. I've been working on the list, or ones just like it, on and off for almost three years now. I'm no closer to an answer and it's gotten to the point where the constant back and forth is just frustrating.

Everyone thinks I should do something different. Coach says to try to go pro, that I can always go to school later. My mom demands I go to college and insists that sports are a hobby not a career. Spencer says to do what makes me happy. Lizzie ... I don't know what Lizzie would say. It isn't the kind of thing I'd talk to her about.

I feel like, at sixteen, I should know what I really want out of life. It's just that none of what I want seems to be stuff I can get just by deciding to have it. I mean, I want to play ball. I want to be someplace with Spencer and Lizzie. And I want to get to know Ally.

Speaking of which...

I flip the paper over and there's another list.

This one is filled with buzzwords. Just in case anyone finds it, I don't want them to know what it is.

It's filled with stupid stuff. Stuff I know about Ally.

I know she can juggle. I know she has one of those big, drooling, Saint Bernard dogs that's almost bigger than she is. And I know, from sitting behind her at assembly last year, that her hair smells like vanilla cookies. That smell doesn't make me hungry, though; it makes me feel a lot of other things that make it difficult for me to eat cookies in public.

The whole thing probably sounds kind of stalkery. But it isn't like that. I mean, I don't follow her or sit in the tree outside her house or anything. I'm not a pervert, just a chickenshit.

I should have talked to her right after she transferred to Maple Grove, but I didn't. After that it was too late to do it without some sort of explanation. Now, over a year later, I'm too embarrassed to even attempt to explain all the times she's caught me staring at her. So the only conversations I have with her are in my head.

Maybe this will be the year I change that. Who knows? Maybe I can use the same visualization techniques Coach has us use for baseball. In those, I picture myself in the field, scooping up the ball and making perfect throws every time. And usually, on the field, that's just what I do.

So now I try to picture myself going up and talking to Ally. I say something witty and memorable, and she smiles at me. I ask her to go out with me and she says there's nothing she'd like better.

"Mr. Ryan?"

Mr. Brooks is standing over me with his arms crossed, looking down at the list I'm trying to bury under my copy of Poe's "The Tell-Tale Heart." There's a wave of laughter behind me. I get the feeling he's called my name a few times.

"Sorry," I say and duck my head down. It's a good bet my face is at least seven shades of red. I'm glad it's Brooks, though, because I know at least one teacher who would have made me read the list out loud to the class.

"Don't be," Mr. Brooks chuckles. "You just volunteered to be our first reader today. Page twenty-two please."

THREE

Maple Grove is split into two towns. The creatively named Main Street divides the kids on the West, who have cars and nice clothes and end up as school president, from those on the East, who bike for miles, shop at Goodwill, and take care of their younger siblings while their parents work second jobs.

The coolest thing on the East side is the monastery, while the West side is dominated by the equally creatively named Maple Grove High School, home of the Mighty Mustangs. The school was the recipient of an influx of money when it was built in the 1950s, complete with bomb shelter, Olympic-sized swimming pool, and a theater to rival any in downtown Detroit. The '60s brought in a planetarium and the '70s a radio station. Then everyone moved out of town and it pretty much went to hell.

Okay, not totally. Enrollment might be a third of what the school can hold, but elementary school kids are still brought to the planetarium on field trips, the radio station has been converted for cable broadcasting, and we still have a kick-ass drama department. And for the three years Spencer, Lizzie, and I have been at Maple Grove, the shining star of that department has been Spencer Yeats.

Tonight we're celebrating not only Spencer's opening night of a showcase called "Songs in the Grove," but also Lizzie's birthday. I'm not sure who first came up with the idea, but somewhere along the line we agreed that the only way to celebrate both events is by breaking and entering, or, in this case, by staying in the school overnight.

But first, Spencer has to get through his show. And Lizzie and I have a surprise for him.

We sit in the center of the front row of the school auditorium and wait, and wait, and wait until *the* song begins. It's the one Spencer performs alone on a dark stage with just a spotlight shining down on him.

Even though Spencer can be one of the funniest people I know, the solo he's been given is serious, sad, and introspective. And because there's no one else onstage when he's singing, it seems to be the perfect opportunity for us to … assist him. Lizzie made a bunch of decorated cue cards with new lyrics on them. I tried to keep her from making them too pornographic, but only succeeded to a point. Honestly, I think they're freaking hilarious.

The stage clears and Spencer walks out dressed in black pants and jacket over a white shirt. If I dressed like that I'd look like a waiter, but somehow Spencer makes it looks pretty cool.

The music kicks in and we let him get through the first verse. For a second I hesitate. He's so good I don't really want to risk throwing him off. Honestly, Spencer Yeats is the best singer I've ever heard that I didn't have to pay to see and probably better than most of the ones I *have* paid to see.

But nothing makes Lizzie falter. She holds up the first card and it takes a minute for him to see it. The corners of his mouth lift. Then he goes on singing about regret and lost love, choices and consequences.

She holds up the next card, which suggests that the guy Spencer is singing about and his mother are having a very un-mother/son relationship. Spencer wanders to the other side of the stage, but when he turns to come back, I can tell he's fighting with himself to keep from cracking up. He's been doing the performance thing for a long time, though, and knows all the tricks. When he closes his eyes, he's back in character.

Finally the song ends and Lizzie runs out of cards. Spencer gives me a smile and a relieved wink and the stage fills again with the rest of the ensemble. My shoulders relax when I realize we didn't get caught, and that Lizzie doesn't seem to have anything else planned, and I can sit back to enjoy the rest of the show.

———————

After the curtain call, Lizzie and I head backstage. "It's your fan club," Laura, one of the other singers, calls out. Everyone else is rushing around, changing clothes, scraping off stage makeup.

I always hate coming backstage. It's like seeing how a magician does his tricks. But there's no way we're going to pull off our whole plan to spend the night in the school unless we're back here, so I have no choice except to play along.

Spencer is still in costume when he lifts Lizzie off the floor and spins her around. Her skirt swirls around both of them like a cloud of dust. I watch, looking for something I'm not sure I'd recognize. Some sign that things have changed, I guess. Some sign that their one night stand, or whatever you want to call it, has irrevocably altered our years of friendship. It doesn't matter how hard I look, though; I can't see anything apart from the close connection they've always had. That *we've* always had.

"You're such a little delinquent," Spencer says with a huge smile on his face. "I thought I was going to lose it." Lizzie laughs in that way only he can make her when he puts her down and slings an arm around my neck.

"Nice, Cal." He ruffles my hair in the same annoying way my mom does and I lean around him to look in the mirror and make sure it isn't sticking up all over.

Then he whispers in an ominous voice, "By the way, when *is* opening day again?"

My stomach clenches. "Sometime in 2050." I wince. I might have had fun tonight, but at some point he's going to get me back and my teammates aren't known for having the same sense of humor as Spencer's drama friends. I just hope whatever he dreams up—a plan that no doubt Lizzie will be more than happy to participate in—doesn't take place during a game.

Spencer laughs as he changes into jeans and a T-shirt that says *I Can't. I Have Rehearsal.* As usual, modesty isn't a theatrical trait because kids, boys and girls both, in various states of undress seem to be rushing around everywhere. I try to keep my eyes forward to avoid looking at Laura's bare back or at Ally as she slowly corrals her long sun-streaked hair into a ponytail.

I don't really succeed at minding my own business and I'm not sure I want to. Standing here, so close to Ally, makes me feel like someone has sucked all of the air out of the room. I'm sure I'd be standing in a puddle of Cal-drool if it weren't for Lizzie urging me, under her breath, to go talk to Ally, to ask her out, to do things whose mere suggestion is making me blush.

For one brief second, Ally glances over her shoulder and our eyes lock. Whatever Lizzie is saying is eaten by the buzzing that overtakes my brain. I'm completely frozen in place. Unable to move. Pretty much unable to breathe.

Eventually, Ally moves away and it takes a minute for me to realize I'm just staring at a now-empty space. I stand there numb and mute while Spencer jokes around with the rest of the cast and crew, who start leaving one by one.

"Noon tomorrow," calls out Mr. Brooks, who isn't only our English teacher but head of the drama club.

"We're running through a couple of those tricky dance numbers," Spencer explains as we follow him to the door. Then, over his shoulder, "See you, Mr. Brooks. Cal and Lizzie are going to help me put all this stuff away." He gestures to the pile of discarded clothes. "And then I'll lock up."

All three of us hold our breath, expecting Mr. Brooks to come up with some reason why we can't be here, but instead he nods and ushers everyone else out of the room. We quickly clean up like we promised and then slink down the stairs to a windowless little basement theater affectionately known as The Cave. The Cave is where the more alternative student productions take place. The name comes from the fact that the stage, walls, floor, and seats are painted black. Everything in the room is formed by moving around a series of identical cubes.

As soon as we get in, Spencer locks the door from the inside. I open my backpack and start taking out a load of candles I borrowed from my mom's strangely endless stash.

"You're sure this is a good idea?" I ask no one in particular. In my head I'm making a list: fire, alcohol, trespassing. I'm pretty sure we're breaking every rule the school has. I wonder how long they can legally suspend someone; there must be laws about that sort of thing.

"I promise we aren't the first to spend the night here," Spencer says. I watch as he grabs a cooler from under one of the black cubes and starts pulling out bits of food. "Just mind the ghost."

Not surprisingly, this gets Lizzie's attention. "What ghost?" Unlike the slightly sick feeling I get at hearing that this place is haunted, she looks excited about it. *Figures.*

I glare at Spencer. I'm pretty sure he didn't mention this particular detail earlier. He knew I wouldn't have come had I known that The Cave was home to a ghost.

Spencer just shakes his head, obviously appalled at our reactions. "Come on, guys. You can pretty much bet that all theaters are haunted."

"Yeah, it's all you angsty theater types who stick around because you're afraid of leaving and having to find real jobs," I say. He throws a roll at my head, which I whip back at him. If I had more control I'd be a pitcher instead of a short-stop, but it's good to know I can throw a roll when I need to. It whizzes by his head and he just manages to duck so that it bounces off the wall.

"When you boys are done acting like boys, can someone fill me in here?" Lizzie lights the candles, each one casting more and more interesting shadows against the black walls.

Spencer sits on one of the blocks, his eyes flashing in the candlelight. He's in his element, getting to tell a story to an attentive audience. I'll be the one who won't be able to sleep, afraid of what might be haunting the place.

"In the late '70s, there was a sophomore named Alice Tyler. She had the lead in *Romeo and Juliet*," Spencer begins in his hushed actor voice.

"Why do these stories always start out with Shakespeare?" Lizzie asks, her voice bouncing loudly off the empty walls. "I mean, we're meant to think he was the greatest writer of all time, but doesn't it seem like every traumatic theater story starts out with Shakespeare?" I know she's baiting Spencer. He knows it too, but can't resist.

"Shakespeare *is* the best," he insists. "But Alice's problem wasn't Shakespeare. Right before the show opened, she found out she was pregnant. And then her boyfriend left her. I don't think that was Shakespeare's fault." He gives Lizzie the same look Mr. Brooks gives kids when he's confiscating their cell phones for texting in class.

"Okay, okay, don't get your knickers in a twist. I was just wondering," she says, but I know she's joking.

"Anyhow ... " Spencer gives Lizzie a look that's all eyes and makes it clear further interruptions won't be appreciated. In return, she sticks out her tongue at him. He continues.

"Anyhow … of course, the show sucked. She broke down crying halfway through the balcony scene and they had to bring the curtain down. The rest of the cast was apparently sympathetic, but the director was a total jerk to her. The next morning, they found her hanging from that rafter."

Personally, I don't really care one way or the other about Shakespeare. I'm just thinking about Alice and how horrible it must be to feel so alone that the only thing you can think to do is off yourself.

Spencer points towards the corner of the room. I can see how Alice would have climbed up on the black boxes and jumped. In my mind I can see her legs kicking under the hem of her skirt.

"Gee, Yeats, you really know how to throw a party." I swallow down the lump in my throat. "I feel all warm and cheery now." I try to turn it into a joke. But I'm really hoping Spencer will take my hint and drop the story. More than that, I want this prickly feeling on the back of my neck to stop.

"Sorry," he says. I also hope he remembers how much this stuff freaks me out. In seventh grade, he brought his brother's Ouija board over and I couldn't sleep for a week after he and Lizzie tried to contact the spirit of her dead grandmother. Knowing that Lizzie was moving the pointer didn't even help to make me feel any less unsettled.

"They say Alice haunts this place. Things get moved around all the time and there are problems with the lights. People have camped out here specifically to try to see her." He finishes his story quickly, the words all flying out in one breath. "And some apparently have."

I look over at Lizzie. She's clearly into the story, probably planning some ghost-hunting expedition to try to lure Alice out of the grave. I vow to keep one eye open at all times, not only because I don't really want to see a ghost, but because I don't trust Lizzie not to try to scare the hell out of me just for fun.

Then they exchange a look that makes the hair on the back of my neck stand up even more than the ghost story did. I can't seem to keep from watching them and cataloging each glance they share and the way they always seem to be touching, like planets orbiting each other.

I get up and go over to the cooler, tapping Spencer on the shoulder on the way over. "Come on, let's see what you brought. I'm starving."

Spencer follows and brings out a plastic Tupperware thing and takes the top off. Six individually decorated cupcakes sit nestled in their own spaces. Each has a theme. One has tie-dye frosting and a little peace sign drawn on it, one is green with little white squares that I assume is a baseball diamond, one has the drama/comedy masks on them, and so on. Leave it to Spencer never to do anything halfway.

"Nice, Betty Crocker. That isn't clichéd or anything," I say sarcastically, but really I'm damned impressed and hungry to boot. My stomach rumbles and both of them laugh.

"Hey, not like you were going to bake her something," Spencer shoots back.

"Yeah, I could have made birthday toast," I admit. "Or maybe scrambled eggs." My parents both have crazy work schedules. I don't remember the last time they were both home to eat dinner at the same time much less show me how to cook it. Recipes in my house consist of mixing something from Whole Foods with something that can be delivered.

Spencer grabs a corkscrew out of his bag and hands it to me along with the bottle of wine. "Here, do something useful." I take them, but I fumble around for a little bit before Lizzie grabs them out of my hands and opens the bottle herself. She has a lot of experience with this sort of thing given that drinking is her mom's favorite hobby. Still, it creeps me out to see her in action.

Spencer sticks glittery little candles into the cupcakes while Lizzie pours red wine into three glasses. I look at Spencer because he's the word guy and I'm sure he's prepared something to say.

"You guys are my best friends in the entire world and I don't know what I'd do without you. Anyhow, I'm so glad we're doing this and, Liz, that you wanted to spend your very special seventeenth birthday with us. I hope you know how much we love you."

She does a little curtsey and hugs both of us while trying not to spill her wine. Spencer goes to the back of one of the black cubes and pulls out three sleeping bags. Then we light the candles and sing happy birthday.

Singing with Spencer Yeats is like singing with John Lennon or someone. I can't even take my tone-deaf voice seriously so I kind of mouth the words and let him carry it until he slaps the side of my leg with the back of his hand. I let go on the "happy birthday dear Lizzie" part just as she blows out the candles.

"So what did you wish for?" I ask, even though I'm not supposed to.

"I want this," she says, looking very sincere and not like herself at all. "I want this never to change."

There's a pause while we both stare at her. I know we're both thinking about how much she must be feeling to actually say that. And then, as if we're sharing the same mind, Spencer and I lean in at the same time and hug her.

————————

Who knew that they turn the freaking heat off in schools at night? I'm sure some people might have thought about that, but not us. I have a light jacket with me and Spencer is in a thin T-shirt. Lizzie is wearing something gauzy and fairy-like that definitely isn't warm.

We pull the sleeping bags together and huddle inside them, each holding candles to keep our hands from shaking. The wine helps a little, but we're almost done with the bottle and I think shivering is keeping me unfortunately sober.

I get up and grab another cupcake. "So when did you find time to make these?"

"I stayed up late last night," Spencer says. "I was waiting for an email anyhow." Lizzie and I share a look; neither of us has to ask who it was from.

After telling us for years that he was "just too busy to worry about relationships," Spencer met a guy from Seattle when they were in a show together last summer. Because of the distance, they aren't really involved, but from what

Spencer told me Rob has been trying to change that. Spencer has been resistant in a cagey, un-Spencer-like way, and I know we won't get any more details out of him tonight.

"Well, thanks," Lizzie says and leans over to kiss him. I force myself not to look away and when she shivers, I throw her my coat.

Spencer collects most of the candles and puts them in the middle of the room. There's one bunch he's left in the corner and I stare at them, trying to figure out what makes them different until I realize they're those little LED candles that won't burn out. They'll stay lit all night long.

It isn't as if I'm afraid of the dark. It's more the things that hide in the dark that get to me. I mean, I'm sixteen; I know there are no monsters under the bed. But there's other stuff that makes the hair on the back of my neck stand up and my stomach clench: ghosts, aliens, predators, muggers, all those parts of our brains that we don't use and don't know why we have, things that can't be explained by science or by reason. It's the not knowing that makes me feel like a silly kid who needs his mommy to leave on the light. I hate that I'm like that, but I am and my best friends know it.

Spencer motions for us to gather our sleeping bags around the real candles, the ones that *will* burn out in the middle of the night, but that also might share some of their warmth with us first.

"Come on, Liz," he says, pulling her over and rubbing his hand up and down her goose-bumped arms. "You're freezing. You're like the walking dead." They unzip their bags and then zip the two together into one giant one and huddle under it.

This is what happens when you're three best friends. Two are always together and one is always on the outside. Not that I want to be in there with them. And not that it's a bad thing. Spencer and I jog together and Lizzie most decidedly doesn't exercise for exercise's sake. Or she and I bum around art museums and I listen to her tell me why people like paintings made up of tiny dots or the tragic stories about the painter's lives. So when they huddle up together, I don't feel left out. Not really. This is just what happens.

Or what happened.

Now that I know they've had sex, everything feels different. I don't want it to matter, but it does. Not just because I feel like they're forming a club I'm not invited to join, but because Spencer should have known better and I'm not really sure how to call him on it. Or if I even should.

"Do you think we'll see her?" Lizzie asks me.

"Who?" I ask, distracted.

"Ally Martin," she answers and I'm glad that they can't see the expression on my face. "No, you know..." She pauses for effect. "The ghost."

"ARGH," I say and put my hands over my ears like a little kid. "I'm not listening." I'm only half joking, but I'm not sure which topic I want to avoid talking to Lizzie about more.

"Give him a break, Liz," Spencer says. "Besides." He points at the LED lights. "That's what the ghost lights are for."

"The what?" Lizzie turns to him. It's clear she's not buying this at all.

"Ghost lights are the lights left on in theaters after the cast and crew have gone. They're meant to keep the muse in the house when there aren't shows going on and keep bad spirits out when there are."

Lizzie's face contains every color of fascination now and she doesn't see Spencer turn and wink at me.

"They're also so that people don't trip over things when they come back to the theater in the morning," he explains.

This practical explanation makes Lizzie smirk, but she says "fine" to him and then mouths "wimp" dramatically in my direction.

Spencer brushes some hair out of Lizzie's eyes and puts his arm around her. "So you're sure your mom didn't have anything planned for your birthday?"

It's a sensitive subject. When we all met in first grade, I remember her mom coming to pick her up from school and knowing there was something wrong. Her dad ran off right after she was born and her mom went through a series of crappy relationships until she settled on the loser she's with now. Even at seven I knew that the smell of alcohol and her unsteady gait made her mom something different, something bad. The idea that she would have planned anything for Lizzie's birthday was pretty absurd. She never had before. She wasn't going to start now.

"Wow, Spence. No more wine for you, it's making you hallucinate," Lizzie says and elbows him in the ribs. "Yeah, Mom had a huge party planned with ponies, and a Ferris wheel, and fireworks."

Spencer winces. I know he wasn't trying to hurt her. It's just hard to tell where all of Lizzie's unprotected nerve endings are; they seem to move around a lot. I can't tear my eyes away as he squeezes her tighter and whispers "sorry" so softly I can barely hear it.

She takes a gulp of wine. "What? It's no big deal. Not like I expected anything from her. Besides, what could she possibly give me that would be better than freezing my ass off with my two favorite boys?"

"I don't think anyone has ever said that they prefer me to a pony before," I say, trying to lighten things up. "I'm not really sure how to take it."

"Oh, Cal." Lizzie purses her wine-stained lips and while I don't know exactly what she's thinking, I know that it's something that would make me squirm if she said it out loud. "I am so not even going there."

I catch Spencer's eye and we dissolve into cold, tired laughter. For the moment, my questions and fears, my doubts and jealousy, fade and all I can think is: this, this, this. This is right.

FOUR

I wasn't made for standardized tests. Spencer is all over these things, but then all of his life has been about studying lines and regurgitating them at exactly the right time. I'm better at stuff like science because the answers are always the same. If you mix chemical one and chemical two they'll always react the same way even if that means you've created something that will blow up. The point is you *know* that's going to happen. The planets tonight will be just where you left them last night so long as you take into account the Earth's slight rotational shift.

But they can ask virtually anything on those tests and I can't possibly study everything to prepare. And don't get me started on writing essay questions for the English part of it, where the right answer is a totally subjective thing based on what the person reviewing the answers had for breakfast that day or whether they got laid the night before.

In reality there's only one good thing about taking the SATs today, on a Monday no less. It means that we're exactly one week from the official start of baseball practice. My Detroit Tigers' calendar, the one with the pictures of the 1968 World Series team, hangs on the wall. I have all our practice times highlighted in yellow on the little calendar squares. The SAT reminder sits in somber black in today's space, right over that first practice. From then on my calendar is full of baseball, baseball, and baseball.

But I have to get through this version of hell first.

I throw my last-minute study notes in the trunk, crank up the radio, and head over to the school. When I pull into the parking lot, it's filled with a large chunk of the junior class. Half of them, like me, are checking their scribbled notes, trying to memorize things they somehow forgot to learn in the previous sixteen years.

All of them look dazed, and tired, and like they'd rather be anywhere else.

Spencer and Lizzie show up with coffee for me, but still I sleepwalk through the rest of the waiting, and the instructions, and then, somehow, the test.

It's all over before I know it.

"Oh come on, Cal, driver picks the music, right?" Lizzie is framed in the rear-view mirror of my car, her dark hair pulled back with a band that has neon flowers protruding off it and an expression of exasperation on her face.

I rub my eyes and some of the stress leaves my shoulders. I feel like I've finally woken up and the day has begun.

Spencer turns around in the seat next to me and smiles because he loves to torture Lizzie. She's going nuts, right on the verge of totally losing it in a manic fury. But she's right. I'm driving, which should give me the right to choose the music, but that's one of the few areas where the three of us are completely incompatible.

Lizzie has a mental block with most music that came out after 1975. "What's the point of popular music?" she always says. "It's all love, blah, blah, heartbreak, blah, blah, shake your ass. No one writes about anything that matters anymore."

Spencer thankfully doesn't want to listen to show stuff because he says he gets enough of that in theater. Instead his poison is public radio, which is almost worse. All talk and news. He says that it gives him perspectives he can draw on when he's acting.

For me, music is music. A beat. Something to fill my head. Something to pass the time. I like the usual—indie rock, a bit of grunge, some old '80s stuff, anything that doesn't put me to sleep.

So it's like this every time we drive somewhere. This battle of wills. I try, but it's torture when I'm driving eighty to have to listen to the news or some droning anti-war song that came out before our parents were born.

Right now Spencer is blaring NPR. The mellow voices discuss a war in some country I've never heard of. It's almost enough to numb my exhausted brain and lull me back to sleep, but for some reason, it makes Lizzie more hyper and she's drumming her hands on our headrests like a bored toddler. I take my eyes off the road for a minute to silently plead with Spencer to do something, anything, to make her stop.

He nods and fiddles with the buttons until he finds something country that we all hate. Without missing a beat, Lizzie smacks him on the back of the head. I would have beaten her to it, but I'm holding onto the wheel for dear life as every truck in Michigan seems to be barreling down on my tail and my ten-year-old Corolla shakes each time one passes.

Lizzie unhooks her seat belt to lean over the console and fiddle with the knobs. Bob Dylan sings about how times are changing in his nasally voice and she leans back with a smug look on her face.

Spencer rolls his eyes, but I can see him smiling out of the corner of my eye. Before I know it, he twists his body, rolls down his window, and sticks his head out of it like a dog and starts singing. That would be fine. Lizzie and I both love listening to him sing. But for some reason he's chosen to sing the score of *The Sound of Music* and between that, which is intended to annoy us as much as possible, and the drone coming out of the speakers, I'm ready to pull over and lock both of my best friends in the trunk.

I still can't take my eyes off the road, but I figure that I'm not going to be a better driver if my ears start bleeding. I reach out a hand and grab for whatever fabric I can feel on Spencer, jacket I think, and yank him back inside.

"Yeats, I swear I'm going to ram this car into a tree if you don't shut up right now," I yell at him, but I'm not really angry and he knows it.

In fact, he keeps singing. Lizzie joins in, making the yodeling and goat sounds to go with that song about a shepherd and I start laughing and can't stop. I finally give up and kill the stereo all together and let the two of them serenade me.

Eventually, they stop—they've run out of songs that both of them know and Spencer has to save his voice for Wednesday's show—and the car is blissfully quiet. I don't turn the radio back on, hoping we can talk instead.

"So when do we get to find out where we're heading?" Spencer asks, looking out the window as random bits of highway fly by.

"Soon," I say. It's a thing we do. One of us will pick some place hours from Maple Grove—a farm that sells pick-your-own blueberries, a dusty used record store, or an ice cream store that sells bacon-and-egg-flavored ice cream—and we'll drive there for the hell of it. Just to see something new and to do it together.

Today, we're on the way to a place called Mystery Ridge where gravity is supposed to be all messed up. It's an old shack where you can drop a ball and watch it roll uphill. Brooms there stand on end by themselves. At least that what the web page I found says.

"I know," Lizzie pipes up. "Let's play truth or dare."

Her words hit me like a jolt of espresso. "No. Not with you, Lizzie, no way."

"Aw, Cal." She draws out her words in a way that makes my stomach clench. "Why not?"

I risk moving my eyes to glance at her in the rear-view mirror. "Why not? First, we're in a car." I don't even want to think of the types of dares she could come up with on a freeway. "Second … how about because last time we played you almost got me arrested."

Spencer laughs. He's safe because he doesn't have anything he really considers a secret from us and always answers all the "truth" questions. I'm always stuck between choosing to talk about things I don't want to talk about, and doing things that I don't want to do. Lizzie, of course, always takes the dares, which we can never make challenging enough for her.

"See, if you'd just answer the questions, it would be so much easier," she says. She's right except that the kind of questions Lizzie asks are hard. Really hard. The type of questions that maybe I think about when I'm alone, but certainly not the type that I can answer out loud. Not even to my best friends. Not to Lizzie.

"Probably," I admit. "Let's try this instead. What do you think you'll be doing in five years? And what about twenty?" Taking the SATs and all this talk about college prep at school has made me think about this kind of stuff lately. And now that I know about Spencer and Lizzie, it feels like everything is changing too quickly.

"Fine." Lizzie sulks. "But you go first and you aren't allowed to say that you want to be married to some girl you can't even work up the courage to talk to."

"I'm totally ignoring that," I say. But really I'm more than happy to skip the topic of girls in general and Ally in particular. "In five years I want to be playing for the Yankees. Or at least their Triple-A team."

"Ha!" Lizzie says. "You are definitely not a bad-ass New Yorker. Doesn't Florida, or someplace slow like that, have a team? That's more your speed." She's right, but hey, it's the Yankees and if you're going to dream, you have to dream big.

"I hate Florida," I say and throw out the one thing that will shut her up. "Besides, Yeats is going to be in New York and you can come out and work for a gallery or something and we'll all be together."

"Okay, so in twenty years you'll be retired on your huge baseball salary with your two World Series rings. What then?" Spencer's optimism is cool, but my mom would be pissed to hear that no one's guesses for me include college.

I'm really getting into the idea of going to college later.

In twenty years, I'll be thirty-six. That's a whole other life away and it's kind of like imagining whether we'll have jet-packs and vacations on Mars by then. I've actually been thinking about this, but am almost embarrassed to say what's on my mind. Then I say it anyhow. "I think I'd like to study meteorology."

Neither of them says anything for a minute, presumably because they're trying to figure out what I'm talk about. Eventually it's Spencer who gets it first. "A weatherman?"

Lizzie starts laughing. "Like on the TV news? The guy who says it will snow and then, when it turns out to be eighty degrees, has to apologize and say that the low pressure system moved or something?"

I search for words that might win them over. I really want Lizzie, in particular, to get it because otherwise she's going to ride me mercilessly. "There's more to it than that. I mean, you can figure out the best flight plans for airplanes or study the chances of hurricanes. There are a lot of options."

"You can plan ahead, you mean?" Spencer manages to sum up my entire psyche in under a minute. "Yeah, makes sense."

Before they can analyze me any further, I pass the question along. "We all know where Yeats is going, so you're up, Lizzie."

She's quiet for a minute. Out of the corner of my eye, I see her lean forward and grip onto Spencer's headrest.

"Well, in five years…" she begins. I twist my head as much as I can and still watch the road. I'm eager to know where she wants to go from here. Lizzie rarely talks about the future.

"I want to be someplace other than this shithole. I want to be able to paint full time. I'm not really sure how to make that happen."

"And what about in twenty?" I ask.

This time there's no pause. She stares right into my eyes in the mirror, deadly serious. "Come on, Cal, do you really think I'll still be alive in twenty years?"

I have to stop myself from jamming on the breaks in the middle of the freeway.

"Liz," Spencer says, before I can get a word out. "Really?"

"Yeah, really. I mean, what? You see me settling down and having kids and a normal life? I don't even know what a normal life is like." She doesn't say any of this like she's upset. Just resigned. It must be hell to go through every day thinking that life is never going to get any better. It makes me think of Alice, the "ghost" from The Cave.

I glance over at Spencer, who looks like all the air has been forced out of his lungs.

"Liz. Do you really think that we'd let anything bad happen to you?"

When he says it I feel a crawling up my back that makes me shiver. That's the kind of tempting-fate comment that made my grandmother knock on wood and spit on the ground.

"Seriously, Lizzie," I say, "you're going to be a beautiful, artsy, bitchy old lady with equally beautiful, misbehaved kids who are afraid of nothing."

That at least brings a smile to her face.

"You're up, Yeats," I say, but we all know his plan. His

life stretches ahead of him like the freaking yellow brick road complete with lion and wizard.

Lizzie jumps in before he gets a chance to answer. "In five years, Spence will be accepting his second Tony award for best male lead on Broadway. In twenty, he'll be living in California with one of the top movie studio executives and a slew of servants in their gated estate. They'll throw parties where champagne runs out of the faucets and everyone is beautiful, and creative, and insane. But in a good way."

Spencer laughs, but really, she probably isn't that far off from the truth.

I blink and then swerve a little. The conversation woke me up, but Lizzie's bleakness about her future has worn me out.

"Are you sure you're okay to drive?" Spencer asks.

"I'm fine, Yeats. And it's still better than letting one of you drive." Spencer drives like my grandmother and Lizzie drives like a demon from hell is chasing her.

Spencer and Lizzie start their usual tug of war over the radio again and I smile at how comforting and familiar it is. I try to look over at Spencer, but Lizzie is leaning between us and I catch a whiff of patchouli before I glance up and see 3,507 pounds of gray steel flying towards us over the median.

Despite what I've read, my life doesn't flash before my eyes.

Time doesn't slow down.

I'm not able to process why an SUV is blocking out the clouds.

I don't have time to utter a sound before everything goes dark.

FIVE

Everything hurts. I'm screaming so loudly I'm pretty sure I woke myself up. I figure out quickly that the screaming must just be in my mind because there's a tube jammed down my throat. There's a machine near me that's making noises that sound like sucking. I know from watching all those hospital TV shows that it's a ventilator and it's breathing for me.

Which brings up the questions, "why aren't I breathing for myself?" and "where the hell am I?"

I try to move, but my arms are pinned down and my chest feels like it's being stood on by an elephant. Everything in the room seems to be beeping and clanging. I'm drowning in sound, and pain, and fear.

The only thing that doesn't hurt is that someone is holding my hand. I move my eyes slowly, and I'm rewarded for the effort by seeing Spencer standing next to me, a blue paper gown over his clothes and a yellow mask over his mouth. He looks bruised, like he's been in a bad fight.

But then he tears up and I have to wonder what's going on that's so bad it's making Spencer Yeats cry. A nurse pushes him out of the way and shines a bright light in my eyes. My back arches with a burst of pain that feels like fire surging through my chest. I want the nurse to go away. I want Spencer to come back and tell me what the hell is going on.

I inhale that horrible antiseptic hospital smell and

wonder if someone is playing a joke on me. I don't remember being sick. I just remember driving.

And then another memory starts to sneak in, slowly at first like it isn't sure it wants to be remembered. I can't quite get my mind to hold onto it. There's something big—really big— coming closer and closer, and then everything goes black. But there's also something else that keeps slipping away; something warm and wet, and it's climbing inside me like a nightmare.

The nurse fiddles with tubes and bags, and puts a pump with a button in my hand and tells me to push it when the pain gets too bad. I'm not sure how to judge "too bad." All I know is that I feel worse than I ever have, even after I tore a tendon a couple of years ago sliding into third. I push the button and the memory, or whatever it is, lies back down and goes back to sleep. And so do I.

———

The next time I wake up, my parents are here. *Both of them.* For some reason, that makes me even more worried. My parents are always working. Always. I can't imagine what could have happened that would possibly drag them away from their jobs when nothing else ever has, including my junior high graduation (Mom had to take a deposition), my Little League championship ceremony (Dad was on a business trip), and parent-teacher conferences (I don't think they've made it to one since third grade).

My usually well-dressed mom looks tired. Her eyes are rimmed with red and I'm pretty sure she randomly picked her wrinkled clothes out of the laundry basket. She has her hand on my forehead like she used to when I was little and sick and she wasn't working in court all the time. It would feel good if it wasn't so unusual. Plus, Dad is standing awkwardly at the foot of the bed and he keeps glancing at the door like he'd bolt if he thought he could get away with it.

The damned tube is still down my throat so I can't talk, but I'm not sure what I'd say anyhow. I don't see Spencer and that makes me wonder where Lizzie is. If something is wrong, she'd be here.

The nurse scurries back; it's a different one this time. This one smells like vanilla and it makes me think of Ally, which makes me wince.

"I know it hurts, honey, but let's try to stay awake for a little bit if you can," the nurse says. I'd laugh if I could, but the nurse doesn't need to know that I'm trapped here in bed aching for a girl I've never spoken to.

My parents are ushered out and a woman I assume is another nurse, or maybe a doctor, positions herself next to me. "We're going to sit you up and then try to take this tube out of your throat, okay?"

It sounds like a great idea until I hear the mechanism for the bed starting up and more pain goes ripping through me. The bed only tilts up a little bit, but it feels like all of my skin has been pulled too tight across my chest.

"Okay, Cal … nod your head if you understand what I'm saying … we're going to wean you off the ventilator to make sure you can breathe on your own."

I want to scream more than I want to breathe, but I

nod and grip the metal railing on the side of the bed, pretending the cool metal is really my mom's hand or Spencer's. In anticipation, I grit my teeth.

The nurse goes to flip a switch on the machine and says, "I'm going to count to three and then I'm going to turn this off. I'm not going to disconnect you until we're sure that you're breathing."

I nod again as she starts the countdown and for some reason it makes me think about baseball. About how you only get three strikes before you're out. About how I have a pretty great on-base percentage. I want to knock this out of the park, but I'm not totally sure what's expected of me. Breathing, I guess. How hard can that be?

I hear her get to "three" and the machine clicks off. I take in air, and let it out, and do it a few more times. She watches like she's waiting for me to do something wrong, but I don't. I just breathe.

After a few minutes the nurse pats my leg. "Good boy," she says, like I'm five or something. "So now we're going to pull the tube out and this might be a little uncomfortable."

Just for the record, I HATE when people use the "royal we." It's fine if you're the Pope or the Queen, but otherwise it really isn't necessary. I made the mistake of telling Lizzie that once and for two weeks Spencer and I had to put up with her walking around saying "we would like lunch now" and "we are having a thoroughly fucking bad day."

The nurse untapes the tube and says, "When I start pulling, I want you to give me a little cough." She pulls, I cough, and my chest feels like it's going to explode as the rubber slides out of me.

I lie back and feel my heart racing. I try to talk, but not much comes out. All I manage is a strangled, "Why?"

"Don't you try to talk too much, Sugar. I'll send your parents in."

I close my eyes. When I open them again my parents aren't there, but Spencer is. He puts his hand on my arm and gives it a little squeeze, but doesn't say anything.

"What is it, Yeats?" I whisper with my scratchy voice. "What happened?"

Spencer looks uncomfortable, like he's found the one circumstance he can't act his way out of.

"I'm not really supposed to tell you. I promised your parents, but I know how you are, and ... " His voice is soft and when he stops, I feel tears press up against the backs of my eyes. I beg: "Please." I can't imagine what he could possibly tell me that would be worse than this not knowing.

He drags a blue chair over, one of the crappy plastic ones they always have in hospitals, and sits down, his hand on my arm.

"We ... we had a car accident."

I try to remember something, anything, and I get that flash again of something flying towards us and that one shard of feeling that something has slithered into me that doesn't belong there.

"Are you okay?" I ask.

He laughs, but it isn't a funny sound. It's a sad one and he turns away. I've never seen him like this, and seeing Spencer in pain is the very worst thing, even worse than being in pain myself and the not knowing what's happened.

"Yeats?" I call to him as loudly as I can, but really it's still only a whisper.

He turns back to me and I can tell from the way that his mask rises that he's trying to smile. "I'm fine. Really. I'm fine. Just a little banged up."

That's all good news; but it's obvious there are things he isn't telling me. Bad things. Things he doesn't want to say and that I won't want to hear.

I open my mouth again to ask about Lizzie, but he cuts me off and rests his hand on my arm. "Cal. You need to take it easy. I'm already going to hear it for telling you about the accident. I'll be back later though, after school, okay?"

"School?"

"Yeah, we're having an assembly." He rolls his eyes.

"What time is it?" I ask, although there are a million questions queued up in my brain and none of them involve the time.

"It's twelve thirty. Lunch time. I just drove over to see you."

I nod and realize how tired I am from talking and wondering. I close my eyes and don't even hear him leave.

SIX

This time when I wake up, there's a party in my room. It's bright and my parents are here with some official-looking guy who stares at me like I'm a puzzle that needs to be solved. I try to keep my breathing steady because every time I start getting wound up, the machines start going crazy.

"I'm Dr. Collins," official guy says. "And I'm going to try to answer some of your questions."

This is what I've been waiting for.

"Your friend told you there was an accident," he says. "Do you remember any of it?"

I wrack my brain again, but it's like there's a big black hole where that memory should be. "No, not really." My voice is a still raspy, but a little stronger than it was when I talked to Spencer. "Just being in the car and then being here."

The doctor nods. "That's normal. People in traumatic accidents often can't remember the incident itself. It's a way the brain has of protecting itself. But if you start to dream about the crash, or remember it and want to talk to someone"—he looks over his shoulder at my parents and I wonder how many conversations they've had while I was out of it—"we can arrange for that. And in fact, if any of the information I'm going to tell you upsets you, we can call someone in here to talk to you or stop for now. Are you okay with that, Cal?"

"Sure," I say, but really I wish he'd get on with it. Across the room, my parents stand like chess pieces with their hands clenched together.

"So, the police report states that the accident wasn't your fault. The driver of the other car hit the median, causing his car to flip over into your path."

I nod again, waiting.

He reads off the clipboard. "When the other car hit you, the airbags deployed, but yours failed. The passenger's bag deployed correctly, which is why your friend only had some superficial lacerations."

I try to focus to figure out what's missing. There's something no one is talking about, but it takes me a minute to realize what that is.

"Lizzie?" I ask. A memory surfaces of her leaning forward from the back seat, almost between me and Spencer. She hates seat belts and the feeling of being constricted. I usually refuse to start the car until she put hers on, but sometimes I just give up. I must have been distracted and didn't think about it.

The doctor looks back at my parents until my mom nods slightly and walks over to my side to take my hand.

"Honey," she starts and then takes a deep breath like I've seen her do before she launches into her closing arguments in court. "Lizzie … was thrown out of the car." She looks over at my dad and closes her eyes. "She was very badly injured, Cal."

I can tell from her expression that she isn't done and I hold my breath, waiting for the kicker.

"She was in a coma. She passed away two days ago."

Two days.

My heart stops and I hear a symphony of machines go crazy around me. I gasp for air, but at the same time, I don't really believe my mom. I've known Lizzie forever. I don't understand the idea of her not being here. Of her not being somewhere.

I wish Spencer were here. I know he'd tell me the truth, that Lizzie is fine. I look around for my phone, but all I see is the doctor stepping closer to me.

"Cal, look at me. I need you to tell me how you're feeling before we go on because there are some other things we need to talk to you about."

How I'm feeling? Is this douchebag serious? How the hell does he expect me to be feeling? I look around the room at everyone staring at me, waiting for me to say something.

"I'm ... " I stop because really, I've had all of ten seconds to process this and I'm just ... I don't even know what. I'm cold. That's what it is. I'm shivering like I'm standing out in the snow. And I can't seem to stop even though my mom is holding my hand on one side and my dad is touching my shoulder on the other.

The doctor looks disappointed. "That's okay, Cal. I'll come back later and we can talk more."

I nod like one of those bobblehead things my dad used to buy me with the huge heads of baseball players on them, the ones you see in the back window of people's cars. I don't really know what else to do.

Dad puts his arm around Mom, and they're looking at me like they don't know what to say either. "We're sorry, champ," he forces out. "I know how close you were to her. How close you all were."

I know he believes what he's saying, but he's wrong. He doesn't know. Spencer and I have spent all this time, years really, looking out for Lizzie. We thought we were keeping her safe. But we failed. After everything we've done—all the late-night calls and trips to get her when things at home got really, really bad—we still failed.

All those times we thought it was her mom and stepfather who were going to hurt her, but now the realization hits me that we were wrong. Although I don't remember the feeling of the car hitting us, what I'm feeling now is much, much worse because what I've realized has edges as sharp as a million knives and it is this: I was the one driving. The one responsible. I killed Lizzie.

––––––––––

"Yeats," I say, even before I'm able to open my eyes.

"Sorry about yesterday," Spencer says. "They keep telling me not to stress you out."

I try to laugh, but what comes out is more of a sad whisper. "You never stress me out," I say and he looks away like he doesn't believe me.

"Tell me. I mean, I need to hear it from you." As I say it, Spencer's face falls and I know. I know.

I ask, "How? Did you see her? I mean, after?"

Spencer turns his head so that he's facing the window, but the shades are drawn and it's dark enough that I can see his reflection in the glass. He takes a deep breath and when he turns back to me, his face is red and flushed like he's been running.

"Yeah. Out there. On the highway. Yeah," he says. "And then here." I know without asking that he isn't going to offer up anything else. I need to ask the right questions if I'm going to learn anything, but at the same time I'm not sure how much I really want to know.

"Was she awake? Did you talk to her?" I try.

He looks at me, chewing his bottom lip like he's trying to find a way to get out of answering. We both know he isn't going to keep anything from me. Not for long anyhow.

"I tried to get you out of the car, but you were pinned down. Some guys from one of the trucks stopped and they told me that we had to wait for the ambulance. They didn't think we should try to move you," he says, shifting his weight from one foot to the other. "I didn't know what to do, so I went to look for her. I talked to her. I held her hand, but..." He rubs his temples and sighs like he's exhausted.

"What day is it?" I ask and he looks both confused and relieved to be asked an easy question.

"Friday. It's Friday."

I have to focus like I'm doing calculus or something. Really focus to figure out what day the SATs were, but eventually I'm able to sort out that it's been four days since the accident. Four days since I killed Lizzie. Two days, they said. Two days since she died. Two days that she'll never have. Four days. The numbers tumble over and over in my head, making it impossible to think straight.

"I'm so sorry," I squeak out. "I'm so sorry." There seems to be so much that I should be saying, but I can't think of anything else besides how damned horrible I feel, and how I want to go back into that medicated ocean and drown and offer my life for Lizzie's. I know I can't make that trade, though, and that I deserve every bit of pain I'm feeling.

Spencer lets me go on like that for a while, but I don't stop until he puts his hand on my arm and squeezes, looking right into my eyes. "What are you apologizing for?"

The answers fly out of me, my mind grasping at anything I could have done to change the outcome. "For not insisting that she wear her seat belt. For driving when I shouldn't have. For killing her. Damn, I'm so, so sorry." Now I'm crying. Sobbing so hard that I think I may never be able to stop.

I can hear the machines start to make their annoying noises again and I try to calm down, taking huge gulps of air, because I don't want the nurses rushing in and mostly because I don't want Spencer to have to leave.

He sits down on the side of the bed and shakes his head. "Lord, Cal … you didn't kill her. Don't even think that. Didn't you hear the doctor? It was the other driver's fault."

I think about putting up a fight, trying to make him realize what I've done, when I get a whiff of the aftershave he keeps for special occasions. That's when I notice what he's wearing: black pants, black sweater, jacket, even a tie. "What are you dressed up for anyhow?"

Spencer looks down and focuses on the blanket on top of me. He runs his hands over the fabric, pulling out little nibs of blue cotton. "I was at," he starts, and then his voice cracks and he clears it and swallows loudly. "Lizzie's funeral," he says softly and raises his eyes to mine.

Of course. They would have had a funeral. It's easy to forget that time in the real world is passing. My days have been filled with swims in the drugged ocean, and pain, and random visits from people in white. But out there, people are going to work and to school. People are having funerals for their best friends.

Even though it was my fault, I have a hard time thinking of Lizzie being dead. I can't stop waiting for her to come barreling into the room, complaining about the hospital food and fighting with the nurses.

"Was it ... okay?" I ask. "I know she wouldn't have gone for any of that sappy stuff from some minister who didn't even know her and ... " I run out of words. Somehow it feels like it I keep talking, none of this will be real, just some play of Spencer's that we're discussing.

Spencer runs his hand through his hair and closes his eyes before wrapping his arms around himself. "It was what it should have been. It was right. I think the whole bloody school was there. It was right and horrible." He loosens his tie and shrugs. "I sang 'Norwegian Wood' of all things. How's that for a funeral song? But I knew it was her favorite."

I remember all the times that I'd heard Lizzie begging him to sing it. I think about how it's a love song but completely unmushy. Just like Lizzie.

He sounded like a fucking angel, too.

My head spins around to see where the voice is coming from, but there's no one in the room but the two of us.

He sounded like a fucking angel, too. The words ricochet through my head and then dissolve like smoke, until it's easy to believe that I didn't even hear them.

"Are you all right?" Spencer stares like he's worried I'm having a seizure.

I strain to listen for any other weird voices but don't hear anything. The meds and the stress must be making me crazy.

"I'm fine," I say. I'm not sure whether I'm trying to convince Spencer or myself. Either way, it's obviously not true.

But he lets it go. "I'm actually glad you weren't there."

"Why?" I ask. It's a really stupid question. Spencer knows I've never been to a funeral. He knows that I probably couldn't have made it through the service without totally freaking out.

He moves my leg over on the bed and his eyes glaze over a little as he talks.

"Because I wish I wouldn't have been there. Because it was the saddest thing I've ever seen. Because all I wanted to do was to throw myself into the ground with her. Because her mom came drunk and because I still can't believe that she's gone." He sounds like he's reciting some lines he isn't sure he's learned yet.

I don't know how to respond. So, instead, I ask another stupid question, the kind of thing that Spencer has always been able to answer. "How are we going to get through this?"

He takes my hand and answers without hesitation. "Together. We're going to get through this together."

I know he means it. It's the same thing he used to say to Lizzie, that we were all together and that she'd always be okay because we were looking out for her. But it turned out to be a lie, so, for the first time since I met him, Spencer's words do nothing but clump together to form a concrete, softball-sized lump in my stomach.

I open my mouth, but I'm afraid to say any of that to him. We've been friends so long that I don't really know how to navigate through everything that's happening if I can't take Spencer's words at face value.

He looks hopeful. He's expecting me to agree, to tell him that someday we'll get over losing Lizzie. I can't push the words out, though. My heart just isn't in them.

So I take the coward's way out. Before he says anything else, I close my eyes and push the button for more drugs and give myself over to the medicated pool. Somewhere, there is a faint and distant lullaby being sung badly off key. I focus on that as I let myself slip off into nothingness and hope that my best friend will understand

SEVEN

I don't want to be awake, but I am. I don't want to hear that I've had a heart transplant, but that's what they tell me. I don't know why they waited to tell me. Actually, that's a lie. They waited to tell me because they were waiting until they thought I could handle it.

And then they must have given up and told me anyhow.

How the hell can you handle the idea of waking up with someone else's heart inside you? It's like being Frankenstein. There are a lot of things in this world you can run away from. Your body isn't one of them.

According to the doctors, my heart self-destructed in a rare and normally fatal series of events. They throw around terms like "traumatic partial aortic rupture," which means that part of my aorta, the largest vein in my body, was almost ripped from my heart in the collision. They talk about the fact that most people die pretty quickly from this. My usual love of stats fails when they start talking about how eighty percent of people who have this happen in a car accident die before reaching the hospital. When they move on to "coronary artery dissection" and "massive myocardial infarction" I tune out and don't even ask them to explain what those mean. All I catch is that I'm "lucky that I'm young" and "lucky that I'm in good shape."

I don't know how they can use that word. "Lucky" is the very last thing I feel.

My parents have been pretty much living at the hospital. We've met with doctors and social workers, nutritionists and physical therapists. It's the most I've seen Mom and Dad since I was in elementary school. And to think, all I had to do was almost die.

The hospital team drills me over and over about what my life will be like. Everything will revolve around exercise, healthy food, routines. It sounds a lot like my in-season regime, until they review the anti-rejection medications I'll need to take for the rest of my life so that my body doesn't think of the heart like the foreign object that it is.

They tell me I'll be on steroids for a year. That on its own means the death of my baseball career in the short term, but I also find out that contact sports could kill me. As a varsity shortstop, there is no guarantee that someone isn't going to slide into me. That I'm not going to have a mid-field collision.

Finding out there's no chance of playing real ball should depress the hell out of me, but I don't feel much of anything. Compared to Lizzie being dead, nothing seems important.

There are visitors in and out of my room: some guys from the team, a few teachers, Spencer, his parents, my parents. I have nothing to say to any of them. I don't know why they're bothering. It's like they won't admit what I've done. I don't deserve their friendship, or their concern, or their love. But still, they parade through my room like spectators at the zoo.

All the time I try to keep a fake smile pasted on my face. I wait for the door to open and for a police officer to walk in and drag me off to jail for killing one of my best friends. It never happens and I don't understand why.

And then there's the voice.

It doesn't tell me to hurt anyone else or myself. It's more like a sarcastic running commentary to what's going on. Sometimes I catch myself laughing in response, which gets me the kind of looks you'd imagine.

It doesn't matter what I do, I can't get it to stop. I even tried not taking my pain meds one day to see if that helped, but all it made me do was cry like a little girl. I can't tell anyone. They'll think I've gone nuts on top of everything.

Maybe I have.

———

On my last day in the hospital, Dr. Collins says he has a surprise for me. I'm expecting him to say that maybe my medical record has been mixed up with someone else's and I can go back to living my life. Or that Lizzie was found alive somewhere and has been playing a really sick joke on all of us.

Instead, he opens the door to my room and waves a girl in. She's a few years older than me, with pale red rings around her eyes and the look of someone who's been through hell. She's pretty in the same way that Lizzie was. The way that makes you sit up and take notice not because she's so overly beautiful, but because it's clear that she isn't taking any shit from anybody.

I try to cover myself up because I'm lying here in only a stupid hospital gown. Meeting a girl is the last thing on my mind, but still I'd rather not look like some invalid kid.

You'd have thought that Dr. Collins might have given

me some warning, but instead he ushers her in and makes the requisite introductions. He tells me that her name is Jessica and that she had a transplant four years ago when she was my age and that she's part of some new program at the hospital for teen transplant patients. Then he leaves us like some misguided matchmaker.

Jessica pulls up one of the plastic seats. "So what happened to you?"

"What do you mean?"

"Were you sick or ... "

"Car accident," I sputter out. I look around, wondering how to get Dr. Collins to come back in here. I haven't wanted to talk about the accident with the people I'm closest to. I certainly don't want to talk about it with someone I don't even know.

"That sucks," she says, but I get the feeling that she only means it to a point. "I was sick. I was on the registry for three years before my transplant."

"The registry?" It sounds like what people get on when they're getting married and want to make sure that they get the plates with the red flowers on them instead of the blue, and that all of their silverware matches.

Her eyes narrow. Suddenly she looks pissed off. "Yeah, the heart registry. I guess you skipped to the front of that line since you were in an accident."

The way she says this makes me feel like I should apologize to her, but I'm not really sure for what. So I whisper out a "sorry." I'm still not really sure why she's here. I mean, her story is sad and all, but what am I really meant to do about it? I don't have anything left to give to anyone else.

"I was at Hilly then," she says, mentioning a high school a few towns over. "I had this…condition. I would have died without the operation." While she talks, she examines her lavender-painted fingernails. She reminds me of Lizzie talking about her mom, the way that she sounded like it didn't matter, which always meant that it mattered more than anything.

It makes me miss Lizzie with an ache deep inside me in a place I didn't even know existed. I haven't cried since that first night with Spencer, but now I can feel the sting of tears behind my eyes. Jessica must think that my sudden sadness is for her because her voice softens a little bit.

"After the transplant, I was doing okay. You know, it was hard. But I wasn't tired all the time and I could do things I couldn't before. But there are a lot of changes to make. Anyhow, I went off to Central State and that's where my problems started."

I try to push through my thoughts of Lizzie to feel some sympathy for this girl. Normally, I'd want to hear her whole ordeal. I'd want to do something to help. But now I just feel like telling her that I have enough problems of my own, that there isn't enough room in my head for hers too. Miraculously I manage to keep my mouth shut. She must be able to read the confusion on my face, though.

"Look. Do you know why I'm here?" she finally gets around to asking.

I shake my head, relieved to be getting somewhere. "No. Not really."

She looks at me like I'm five and just told her I wet the bed. "I'm your version of 'Scared Straight.'"

I still have no idea what she's talking about, which must be clear from the expression on my face.

"You know … that movie they used to show kids about how bad life in prison was so that they'd behave?"

That doesn't make it any clearer, but this time I decide to play along and fake it. "Right. So you're … "

She's really pretty. But not as pretty as Ally. Still, I bet you could pull her onto this bed and really make those machines go crazy.

I reach up to block my ears from the voice and close my eyes. I'm sure I look like a nutcase sitting here like this, but I don't know what to do to get it to stop.

It isn't even like I even find Jessica *that* attractive. Or that girls are anywhere on my mind at the moment.

"Sorry," she says. "Am I boring you?"

"No." I force my hands down. "It isn't you. No." I can feel my face getting red. It isn't like I can tell her that some voice in my head just said she was pretty and that I should drag her into my bed.

She turns away and starts looking through the cards that are taped up on the wall. Cards from everyone at school. She's looking at one from Spencer that has a bunch of clouds on it and when you open it, it sings about gray clouds clearing up and putting on a happy face. It makes me feel odd to be watching this girl I don't know going through my stuff. I'm relieved when she comes back over to sit in the chair near the bed.

"Look, last year, I went to Florida for spring break with a bunch of friends. I spent a lot of time convincing

my parents that I was healthy enough. And I was. But ... "
Her hands ball into fists.

I can't help myself from being curious now. "But?"

"But one thing led to another. I had a few beers and that was probably bad. But do you know what the worst thing was, Cal?"

It's strange to hear her say my name like she knows me. She's angry. I don't know if it's with me, or herself, or with something else entirely.

I shake my head. "No? What?"

She's pacing now. "We stayed up late every night. And I slept in every morning. I figured what the hell? An hour here or there, I'd be fine. I was sticking to the stupid diet for the most part. I was working out. I deserved a few leisurely mornings, right?"

I nod because it seems reasonable the way she puts it.

This makes her slam her fist on the tray table. The cups of green Jell-O I've been collecting for Spencer, who actually likes them, almost go flying.

"No. Haven't you listened to anything they've told you?"

I feel like I'm taking some pop quiz in a language I've never studied. "I ... "

Her face stiffens. "Listen to me, and listen well because if you don't pay attention to anything else, you need to get this. I slept in. I missed taking my meds on schedule. By the time I got back to Michigan, my body was starting to reject my heart. Do you understand what that means?"

I only have an inkling. The doctors talked to me about the chances of my body rejecting my new heart. My mom said the word "rejection" the way that my grandma used to say the word "cancer," in a whisper like if you didn't say it out loud there was no chance of it happening.

"Do you have a girlfriend?" Jessica asks completely out of the blue. It isn't any of her business, but I shake my head.

She looks at me kind of funny and says, "That's a shame, you're kind of cute," which makes me blush and have to look away. From somewhere far away I hear laughter. I have to sit on my hands to resist the urge to press on my temples again to try to get it to stop.

"Anyhow, seriously, maybe you used to worry about being rejected by girls. Or boys. Whatever you're into. But now your life is going to be about trying to prevent being rejected by this heart. Don't fuck it up."

Jessica stands up and walks to the door, looking way more tired than she did when she came in. Before she steps out, she turns back. "They hate doing transplants on teens, you know. Kids they can train. Adults just resign themselves to following all the rules. But we always think we're smarter than the doctors, smarter than our bodies. And you know what? We aren't. Just remember that."

EIGHT

I'm scrubbing the baseboards of the kitchen floor. Back and forth, back and forth. I can't figure out why it's taking me so damned long until I look down and see that I'm using a toothbrush. This is insane. My parents have a housekeeper who comes once a week. Why am I doing this?

I stand up to ease my cramped muscles and a shower of dark hair falls down my shoulders.

I lurch up in bed. These dreams I've been having since I got home are making me nuts. Stupid me for thinking everything would get back to normal.

On the outside nothing has changed. Nothing, except that I've had to turn the page on my calendar and wipe the dust off my trophy shelf to make my room look normal, lived in. When I got home it looked like Pompeii, that city that was frozen when a volcano blew up and encased everything in dust. Frozen the day of the SATs. The day of the accident.

But on the inside, everything is different. Some days, it's hard for me to picture Lizzie's face. On others, it feels like she's here next to me. Neither is particularly comforting. I miss her. I don't ever want to forget her. It's just that thinking about her makes me feel like I'm going to puke. It reminds me that I'm the reason she isn't here.

I get dressed and head downstairs, massaging my hands, which are cramped from my dream.

Please let Mom have left for work, I pray over and over, but like all of my other prayers these days, this one goes unanswered. Of course it does. No chance that she won't be here on my first day back to school.

When I get to the kitchen I can see that she's already exasperated from the way her hands are wrapped tight around her coffee cup. It's like she wants to turn back the clock and make me her perfect baseball-playing son with a secure future again. And she can't. So instead, she's trying to do the things she can. Only I don't need her to. I don't want her to.

"I'll drive you to school, Cal," Mom says.

"Spencer is picking me up," I tell her for the tenth time since yesterday. "Not that I couldn't have walked the five blocks like I've done just about every day for the past three years," I add under my breath while I sort through the mountain of pills I need to take before I leave.

She leans towards me on the counter and the smell of her coffee makes my mouth water. Caffeine is on my restricted list so I can only inhale the fumes. "You have to tell me what I can say here to get you to take this seriously. It isn't like you've been out with the flu."

That makes me laugh, but it isn't a real laugh. It sounds hollow and bounces around inside my head. I'm not sure I remember how to really laugh.

"I think I know that." I scratch around the incision. As it heals, it's itching, which is one more thing on the list of what's making me nuts. "But I'm supposed to be exercising, remember? Dr. Collins said so." I play the doctor card because now his word is law and if my mom ignores everything I say, she at least listens to him.

Mom sighs, puts her mug down, comes over, and cups my cheek in her hand. She's become a different person since the accident. Someone who remembers she has a kid. But it's too late. It feels like she's suffocating me with her need to know the one thing I can't tell her: that I'm all right.

"I know," she says. "It's just difficult not to worry about you."

I wonder how hard it would be for her if she knew that I was hearing voices. But I don't tell her. Instead, I do what I've always done. I follow the rules and all of the doctor's instructions.

The only thing I've taken a stand on is about going back to school because I have to get out of this house.

My parents are making me prove I can handle all the new rules as a condition for going back, so I've made a big show of hanging a list of reminders over my desk: times to take my meds, things I can't eat, a schedule for working out and how much I can do. I copiously copy each reminder and note onto my calendar in different colors. It looks like a crayon factory exploded in my room.

In the meantime, my parents and the doctors have met with the school administrators. I guess they need to know what I should and shouldn't do and to look out for any signs of my getting really sick. I don't know why that surprises me, but it's the only thing that makes me nervous about going back. All of those eyes watching me, studying me.

"I'll be okay," I say with more confidence than I really feel. "I'll call you at lunch or something."

She nods. "Cal … there's one other thing."

"What?" I'm stuffing books into my backpack, which has sat unused for a month.

"Linda and I," she begins, and I wonder what occasion is prompting her to get together with Spencer's mom. "We're going to go out to the cemetery this afternoon. To plant some flowers on Lizzie's grave."

She looks at me and I freeze, my chem book in one hand and my bag in the other. It isn't like I haven't spent hours thinking of going to school and passing Lizzie's locker. Not seeing her there. Trying to prepare myself for her absence.

I haven't been very successful. It's easier, I've found, to worry about something being added than something being taken away. How do you prepare for something to be missing?

It's funny. I loved Lizzie, but she was like a bomb and you never knew when it would go off or whether it would shoot confetti and streamers all over the place or blow up the building. She filled whatever room she was in. Like a carnival or circus.

I can't handle thinking about that energy being trapped inside a box, lying beneath six feet of dirt. I don't get why my mom doesn't understand that. Not like I was the kind of kid who was into horror films; more like I was the kid hiding under the bed during thunderstorms.

"Mom, stop." I'm on the verge of walking out of the room so I don't have to listen to her talk about Lizzie and graves in the same breath.

She puts her hand on my arm, and it's clear that this conversation is going to happen whether I want it to or not. "I know, Cal. I know this is hard. But you should come with us. It will give you some closure."

I shake my head and pull my arm away as I start shoving things back into my bag. "I don't want closure. I want her back and I can't get that." I pray that this once my mom will turn into one of those comforting TV moms that seem to understand everything. But really, there's little hope of that.

I want…

"You need to find a way to try to accept this," Mom says.

She might as well be speaking Klingon for all the sense that it makes to me. "You don't think I've accepted it? I miss her every second of every day. How much more real do you want it to get for me?" All of a sudden, I'm pissed off and I can hear my blood pounding in my ears. I stalk over to the window waiting for Spencer to show up, feeling like I need to escape.

"Calvin, I could do without the tone." Oh lord, I can't believe she's getting all parental right now. "I know that you miss her. And I know that it doesn't make sense to you, but sometimes seeing someone's grave makes you feel closer to them. It makes it easier to handle the fact that they're gone."

"Really? You think that my going there and imagining her suffocating alone in a freaking box is going to make me feel close to her? You think that's going to relax me and not give me nightmares for the rest of my life? Sorry," I say ramping up the sarcasm. "You must be thinking of your other kid."

I hear Spencer honk, not a second too soon. The sound mingles with my mother's sigh of resignation. As I grab my bag, she comes up and kisses me tentatively on the cheek. I grit my teeth and try not to pull away.

"Some other time then," she says. "Be careful today and call if you need anything."

I leave without saying a word. My head is full of thoughts—of things I want and things I need. None of which anyone can give me.

———————

I throw my bag into the backseat of Spencer's black VW Golf, which he's named "Sweeney" after the musical he did with Rob last summer, and then throw myself painfully and regrettably hard into the passenger's seat.

I kind of expect Spencer to chew me out because he treats Sweeney like it's some piece of expensive artwork and not just a car. Instead he must see the pain that crosses my face because he takes one look at me and asks, "Do you want to talk or should I just shut up?"

I glare at him with what's left of my anger, then manage to relax enough to respond without being a jerk. "Sorry," I say. "It isn't you. My mom is out of control."

"I'm sure she's just worried about you. You can't blame her."

If the world were to suddenly stop spinning and for some reason Spencer couldn't be an actor or singer, he would be a diplomat. Usually it's what I like best about him, that he can see all sides of every issue. He's always calm and rational regardless of the circumstances. But now, it irritates me a little. I want someone to be pissed along-side me. Lizzie would have been great for that. She could always be counted on to join in when you wanted to be angry about something.

"Yeah, fine. But it isn't just that," I try to explain, hoping he might have the same reaction I did. "Do you know what she and your mom are doing this afternoon?"

Spencer keeps his eyes on the road and the hesitation before he answers tells me all I need to know.

"Yeah," he admits. "I wanted to go with them, but we have a full rehearsal after school."

Crap.

"Figures." My anger flares again.

"Look … " he starts, and I realize I've gone too far. My emotions are yo-yoing all over the place and I have to wind them back in. I want to blame that on the steroids. The doctors said crazy feelings could be a side effect, but I know my anger has nothing to do with the meds.

"Sorry. I'm not pissed at you. I just can't do it. I can't go there and imagine her like that. It's making me sick thinking about it." And it is, actually. I'm feeling sweaty and chilled the way you get before you throw up. I roll down the window, hoping the fresh air will keep me from puking all over the pristine interior of Spencer's car.

"No big surprise there." He makes a sound that would turn into a laugh if we were talking about anything else because really, the chance of me going to a cemetery and not completely freaking out is exactly zero. "It does help some people, you know." His words are tentative. He knows he isn't going to win me over.

More forceful is the voice that fills my head. *Like me.* I try to ignore it and focus on Spencer. He's let his hair grow out some since the accident and it's got that shaggy look that Lizzie always loved and it's curling slightly against his white shirt in a way that I could never pull off.

"Cal?" I look up to see him staring at me, concerned. "You okay? You got really quiet."

I close my eyes and then turn to look out the passenger's side window, not sure of what just happened. "Yeah. Yeah, I'm fine. Anyhow, have you gone? To the cemetery?"

"A few times," he admits. "It's actually a really peaceful place. There's a lake and swans of all things. Lizzie would like that."

"What do you do there?" I know as I ask that it's a pretty silly question, but really I don't get it.

Spencer's hands tighten almost imperceptibly on the steering wheel. If I didn't know him so well, I wouldn't even catch the sadness in his voice. "I talk to her. Sometimes. I tell her what's been going on with school. With you. I know it sounds strange but I feel closer to her there."

"Think I'll just take your word for that," I say.

"Everyone has their own way of dealing with things. I'm sure your mom will get that it makes you uncomfortable and ease up."

I know he's trying to help, but suddenly I want, no I *need*, to stop talking about this before I lose it completely. When I look down, my fists are clenched so tightly that they're cramping again. More than anything I don't want to be like this with Spencer.

I try to think of something to tell him that doesn't involve pain or meds or this aching loneliness I feel without Lizzie, without baseball... it's like I don't even know what I have left aside from him. And so I have nothing to bring to the table. "Talk to me about something else. Seriously, tell me about the show," I beg.

For a minute I think Spencer is going to fight and tell me how important it is that we talk everything out, but then he launches into one of his crazy stories about rehearsal for the spring play and within a few minutes, the pure normalness of the conversation makes my heartbeat slow and I've almost forgotten about graves and about one of my best friends being buried under dirt.

NINE

Thankfully, it's pretty easy to be distracted from your thoughts when everyone's looking at you like you've grown a second head.

Half the kids, even ones I don't know and have never really talked to before, want to ask questions. The others ignore me as if getting into a car accident and destroying your heart and your future is contagious.

Trying to get to class on my own is like running the gauntlet when all I want is for everyone to ignore me, to fade into the woodwork. I know they don't look at me as their star player anymore, but I want them to at least stop thinking of me as nothing more than transplant boy. Before I even get to my first class, I'm cornered by Assistant Principal Stiller. He's been assistant principal for a million years. I think it might have been his first job and it looks like he's going to stay in it until he dies. Every time the school starts interviewing for a new principal there are rumors that he wants the job, but he never gets it. This comes as no great surprise to anyone, it seems, aside from Assistant Principal Stiller.

"Calvin Ryan, hold up," he calls as he runs toward me, layers of flesh bouncing in front of him.

I've only told him about a hundred times that I hate being called Calvin. So now, along with my mom, that's twice today, which isn't a really good way to get back into the swing of things.

"Mr. Stiller, I have Chemistry," I say, hoping he'll remember that being in class on time is something he's made a personal crusade. "And I go by Cal," I throw in for good measure, but he looks at me with a blank expression so I let it drop.

"I'll get right to the point, young man. We were thinking of having an assembly." He stands there glassy-eyed as if I'm meant to know what he's talking about.

"Assembly?"

"Yes. What do you think?"

I try to remember if there's something I'm meant to be doing, some project I should have been preparing while I was in the hospital or something.

"Sorry, sir. You've lost me."

His shoulders come up with an exaggerated sigh that hauls his too-small shirt up to expose a ribbon of flesh that burns my corneas. I pull my damaged eyes up to his face, which isn't that much better because he's looking at me like I'm an idiot and he's just going to have to resign himself to explaining what he means.

"We want to have an assembly." He even slows his words and gets louder as if, perhaps, I've gone deaf. "You know, about you and your…" He does that thing with his hands that people do when they don't know the word for something. It looks like he's mixing cake batter and pointing at my chest at the same time.

"Transplant?" I offer.

"Right. That."

He stands there waiting for an answer he isn't going to like. The very last thing in the universe I want is to have a full-school assembly on anything having to do with me. The last time I stood on that stage was when the varsity teams were introduced. I'm not going up there as a loser now.

"You know, I'm not really sure that's necessary, sir." I try to figure out what I could tell him that would guarantee that an assembly won't happen. "In fact, I don't think I'm meant to be in a room with that many people yet." He looks puzzled. "Germs. And, I mean, if I got sick... I'm not sure the school is insured for that. But did you want to check and let me know?"

I'm being a smart-ass and if it was anyone besides Stiller, they'd see right through my act. But he scrunches his face up and shakes his head just as the bell rings, so I give him a smile and duck around the corner.

———————

Thanks to Spencer's notes and the study sheets the teachers sent home, I'm not as far behind in my morning classes as I would have guessed. But still I'm relieved to survive long enough to make it to lunch, even though I had to get to the lunchroom the long way so that I could avoid walking by Lizzie's locker. I wasn't ready to see that yet.

The smell of pizza wafts through the air and my stomach grumbles as I look at the plate of salad with grilled chicken in front of me.

Given the weather, I might normally be running laps or throwing a ball around with some of the guys, anticipating the start of our season. But according to the doctor-approved schedule on my bedroom wall, I'm a week away from even doing something as simple as running laps. So, for the first time in as long as I can remember, I'm eating lunch alone, stuck in here hanging out with salad while Spencer is off at an emergency session to re-harmonize or something.

I have the new *Sports Illustrated* to read through while I try to pretend that I'm eating food with flavor, but even that isn't holding my attention enough to keep me from hearing my name being mentioned followed by a bunch of hand-slapping and wisecracks.

Justin Dillard is sitting at a table by the window with a bunch of no-necks from the wrestling team. I'd be more than happy to ignore them if they weren't being so obvious about high-fiving and pointing at me.

Finally I've had enough of both the salad and being the subject of their conversation, so I roll my magazine up and head over.

"Let's hear it, Dillard. You obviously have something to say to me." I lean towards him with both palms on the table. He gives me a look that would curdle milk. It's an old game between us.

"Yeah, we were just over here wondering..." He lifts his eyebrow, waiting to see if I'm going to take the bait.

I could walk away, but I really want this over with. I can't imagine what he's going to hit me with—questions about the accident? My hospital stint? What?

"Wondering what?" I ask, trying to sound bored. I shift so that I'm leaning on one leg as if I'm really on my way to someplace else.

"You know. If the rumors are true about you and her."

If there are rumors about me hooking up with some girl, then someone in my school has one hell of a sense of humor. "Why don't you try to put it into English, and I'll let you know."

"Shame they couldn't give you a new brain while they were at it, Ryan. We were wondering if it's true that you got Lezzie's heart." That damned nickname, the one Lizzie "earned" by not wanting to go out with him, sets my teeth on edge.

Fuck you, Justin, says the voice in my head at the same time the words come out of my mouth.

Then I stop to try and figure out what he's talking about. "What the hell are you talking about?" I creatively spit out. My shoulders tense. A muscle pulses in my arm.

"My mom heard from Lezzie's mom that she agreed to let them take her heart and give it to you. Guess that was the only way you were ever going to get a piece of her."

The room goes suddenly quiet. It isn't that everyone has stopped talking or clanking silverware. It's my head that's suddenly a black hole of silence and confusion.

Some part of my brain must still be working because I know that trying to explain to Dillard that I never wanted "a piece of Lizzie" is a waste of time. Still, I can't just let it go because seriously, what the hell is he talking about?

"Once again, what the hell are you talking about?" I'm

in his face now. I'm really not a violent person, but I have fantasies about wiping the floor with Dillard.

"You didn't know, did you? I bet they thought not even you'd want to walk around with that weirdo's heart inside you."

I freeze because I have no idea what else to do. My chest is aching and I don't know if I'm going to pass out or worse. I want to defend Lizzie, but this jerk means nothing and I don't want to waste the energy on him and his bullshit.

I want to punch something so badly that I'm shaking from trying to hold it in. I manage to propel myself out of the cafeteria, bashing into a few kids who are standing talking in the doorway, and fall against the brick wall of the hallway trying to catch my breath.

I lower my head and shoulders and lean with my hands on my knees, on the verge of hyperventilating.

"Cal?"

A hand touches my shoulder and I lurch up in full defense mode but it's only Coach Byrne. I'm sure he's less than happy at seeing his once star player losing his shit in the hallway.

"Cal, are you okay?" he asks, all concerned. "Do you need to sit down?"

There was a time, back when I was on the team, that I would have told him everything. But now I'm nothing. I can't play varsity for him this year. I'll probably never really be able to play baseball again. Plus, Coach is going to have to start Justin Dillard at short and the thought alone would make me sick even if it wasn't going to cost the team games. I don't want to make it worse by wasting Coach's time.

I shake my head and force myself to smile and nod at the questions he asks that don't quite register in my brain. I guess I get it right because eventually he leaves. But all I hear in my head are Dillard's words over and over.

Lizzie's heart. Beating inside me. I can almost feel it now. Her. What's left of her. Pushing blood through my body. However much I want to dismiss it, I can't. I know it's true. There's no doubt in my mind and it makes more sense than anything I've heard in a while. I don't know whether to laugh or cry.

But the question is why didn't someone tell me? Anyone. I wonder if Spencer knew. Would he keep something like this from me? Ten minutes ago I would have said that I'd trust Spencer Yeats with my life. But now I don't know.

And what about Mom and Dad? Can I not even trust my own parents?

I glance down the hall to make sure Coach Byrne is gone and make my way to the auditorium. I'm so shaky I have to reach out one hand to steady myself against the wall.

Music seeps out from under the door. It pisses me off that anyone can sing these happy, stupid songs right now. Don't they know how wrong that is with Lizzie gone?

I pull the heavy door open and stand along the back wall, scanning the stage for Spencer. My arms are knotted over the chest that now contains what little is left of Lizzie. I want to hold her in, and at the same time I want to rip my chest open and pull her beating heart out of me. The urge scares me, so I force myself to place each hand behind me on the wall. My nails try to pierce the brick with no luck. But the trying feels good. Unlike me, this wall will not break and I need something that's going to fight back.

I stand there like that, my breath coming in fast, panicked gasps until I see Spencer pull Mr. Brooks aside and bend his head toward me. Mr. Brooks looks at me briefly and then back to Spencer and nods.

Spencer does a slow jog down the aisle and a hundred thousand emotions run through me. He usually makes me feel happy and calm, like I know where I'm meant to be. But my rage at Dillard is still churning and the thought that my best friend would keep something like this from me joins it, making me angrier than I can ever remember being.

Spencer sidles up to me, oblivious to the surging crest of fury that's sitting in my throat and threatening to choke me. Except that he has to know something is up or I wouldn't be here interrupting his rehearsal.

He grabs my arm and looks into my eyes with that sincere, caring expression that is all Spencer, and I just want to fall apart. He isn't upset that I'm here, interrupting his rehearsal. He doesn't look put out or even like someone worried that I've figured out what he's been hiding.

"Are you okay? You look pale," is all he says.

I want to slide down the wall and cry, but I can imagine how that would look; baseball star turned Frankenstein losing his shit in the auditorium.

I must look as bad as I feel because Spencer pulls me back out into the hallway. Kids and teachers are milling around and running back and forth trying to make the most of their lunch hours. They're totally oblivious to us. So I sit down on the hard floor outside the auditorium door.

Spencer sits down next to me, giving me time to catch my breath and figure out how to accuse him of this horrible thing, but I need to get the words out of me as fast as I can. I can't stand being kept in the dark like this.

"Is it true? Did you know?"

"Know what?" he asks, but I can hear the admission in his voice. I don't even have to answer his question. He knows what it would take to make me this upset. I just stare until he closes his eyes.

"Cal…"

"Don't fucking 'Cal' me. Why didn't you say something?" My voice is loud enough to get the attention of a few kids who turn to look at us and then go back to their own conversations and keep walking.

"The doctor, your parents, they said…" Spencer lists the people who swore him to secrecy and then stops. "Who told you?"

"Justin Dillard."

"Right," Spencer says, and sighs. Suddenly the entire thing is clear for him. "Right. His mom runs the bar that Lizzie's mom drinks at. I always forget that. I'm sorry, Cal. I'm really sorry. I wanted to be the one to tell you, but your parents and the doctors really came down on me for spilling about the accident. I was afraid if I said anything they wouldn't even let me anywhere near you."

It's not Spence's fault, the voice in my head insists. Lizzie's voice, I know that now. And I think I've known it all along. *Don't you think this has been hard on him?*

The small part of my brain that can handle being rational

thinks about it and realizes that she's right. It isn't his fault. I'm sure he was pressured into keeping the truth from me. I try to exhale all of the anger at Spencer that I can. He isn't the right person to take this out on.

"Yeah, I get it. Man, it's so screwed up. This whole thing is so screwed up. Yeats, she's inside me. I can feel her sometimes. I've been having these dreams and I swear that they aren't even mine." As I admit that, I realize that I want to tell him about hearing Lizzie's voice, too. But I'm already afraid to see Spencer's expression, worried that he'll think I'm crazy. That he'll call my parents, or the doctor, or some therapist that Dr. Collins suggested I talk to. But it's Spencer, so all he does is scoot over slightly closer to me so that I know he's still on my side.

He sits there while the sounds of the rehearsal seep under the door. He doesn't press me to say anything else, which is good because I don't think I can talk about it. Not even with him.

But of course he says the only thing that could possibly make it okay for Lizzie's heart to be beating inside of me: "That sounds like a Lizzie thing, you know," he says with a forced smile. "She'd like the idea of haunting you."

It makes me smile a little too because it's so true. Lizzie would love the idea of making me squirm for the rest of my life.

I know I should let him go back to rehearsal. He's got the lead and I'm not sure how much they can do without him. My anger at him is gone and suddenly I'm just really, really tired.

Plus there's another conversation I need to have. And not with him.

"Will you pick me up for school tomorrow?" I ask.

He relaxes and smiles with relief, which makes me relax a little too. "Of course. Usual time?"

"Yeah. Thanks." I get up. I'm still a bit shaky and put my hand out to pull him up.

He takes it and looks at me like he's trying to figure out if we're really okay or not.

"Sorry for interrupting rehearsal," I say.

"No, that's fine. I'm sorry for … you know," he says as he turns to the door. "Hey, Cal?"

I just look at him, wondering what he sees now when he looks at me.

"Don't be too hard on your parents."

I can't reply, so I just shrug and turn to walk away.

The thought of going back to class to try to memorize the greatest hits of European History makes me feel like my head is going to explode. Instead I head to Lizzie's locker and stand in front of the gray metal. I reach out and lay my hand on it and it's cold under my skin, which, for some reason, brings tears to my eyes. I grab at the lock and spin the dial to open it. She always used Spencer's birthday as her combination, but then she knew my combo too (6-23-20, the uniform numbers of my favorite Tigers, and Spencer's 22-2-45, the address of his favorite Broadway theater) and we were always in and out of each other's lockers. I only want one thing; I want to see her painting. I want to feel close to her. But as I'm dialing, a picture springs into my head of her shivering in a locker-sized box in the cemetery and I can feel my lunch threatening to come back up.

I drop the lock like it's a line drive and head to the nurse's office to tell them I'm feeling tired—a gross understatement—and think I should go home. I let them poke and prod me a bit. The nurse watches as I call a cab to take me to the house. Mom is in court so there's no chance of reaching her, but they leave my dad's assistant an urgent message that I'm sure will get his attention.

TEN

When I get home I park myself on the couch in the living room, but leave the lights off. For once what I'm afraid of isn't the stuff I *don't* know; it's the stuff I *do* know. I can't say why I didn't think to ask where my donated heart came from. There's been so much going on, so much to get used to. It makes me feel selfish to think I didn't wonder. But that doesn't absolve my parents for not telling me that I was walking around with Lizzie's heart inside me.

The shadows change as the last bits of daylight move across the room. Finally a car pulls up and my dad's keys jangle in the door. He comes in and flips on the light, looking a little bit relieved, like he thought he was going to come home and find me dead on the floor.

"Hey champ, the school called. Are you feeling all right?"

I don't give him a chance to take his coat off. I move in front of him, realizing that we're the same height now. Part of me wants to settle this like a man and take a swing at him. But I can't; he's still my dad.

Instead I push a finger into his chest. Surprised, he backs up against the door.

"Her heart? Of all the people in the world, they gave me Lizzie's heart and you didn't even fucking tell me?" I don't think I've ever sworn at my dad and he looks completely shocked. He tenses and I think he's going to fight back. But then his shoulders slump and he gently moves my arm away.

"Cal. Look."

"No, you look," I say, pacing around the living room like a caged tiger. "She was my friend. One of my best friends in the world. And you and Mom didn't think it was important to tell me that it's her heart that's keeping me alive?" My blood pressure is going through the roof just like it isn't supposed to do and I take a deep breath to try to calm myself until I hear his answer.

"Of course, we know it's important. We know how close you were."

This does it. This pushes me over the edge that I've barely been hanging onto. "No. You don't know. How can you know? Neither of you have really been here enough to know. Did you know that Lizzie's mom was a drunk and allowed her series of loser boyfriends to hurt her own daughter? Did you know that? Did you know that Spencer and I used to go over there and break up the fights and drag Lizzie out of there? Did you know that we've had to take her to the hospital more than once? Did you know that?" The words are pouring out of me like they can't escape fast enough. Blood rushes in front of my eyes. I'm breaking every rule that the doctor gave me and I don't really care if I drop dead here in the middle of the living room. It would serve them all right.

Dad goes pale and looks like he's going to be sick. He's afraid of me and right now he should be.

"We knew her mother drank, but no, Cal. We ... " He fumbles for words, but I don't care what he has to say.

I poke him in the chest again to emphasis each word. "Then. Do. Not. Tell. Me. You. Knew. How. Close. We. Were." I spin around to keep from slamming his head into the wall. I'm shaking and the tears start, but I don't want him to see them. I don't want to be the one who backs down. Not this time. "You didn't know anything."

I stand there, facing the window, on the verge of sobbing, trying to catch my breath. Dad comes up behind me, but wisely doesn't touch me. I feel coiled as tight as a spring. The slightest thing will make all of this anger explode.

"We weren't keeping this from you. We just wanted to wait until you were stronger."

I turn around and clasp my hands together like I used to when I was a little kid and Mom would take me to stores filled with glass things. She taught me to keep my hands away from anything fragile. Anything that can break. Anything I can smash.

Dad stares, pleading with me to understand, to forgive. But I don't. I can't. I've spent a month wondering if I was losing my mind, not able to tell anyone about the dreams and the voices. Figuring that I deserved them after what I'd done to Lizzie. But now I know differently. This is all her. And as much as I try, I'm not a little kid any more. And it's too late to keep me from breaking anything. Lizzie is proof of that.

———

I do my homework and go to bed before Mom even comes home. I turn on the nightstand light and then turn it off, and then turn it on again. It's like an SOS signal, only there's no one out there to see it. For once the light isn't helping. I don't know what to do to keep the shadows at bay when they're already inside me, beating like a badly timed drum.

Stars and planets glow on my ceiling. I put them up there sometime in middle school and never took them down. I spent weeks getting the configurations right and to be honest, I've sometimes wondered what it would be like to make out with a girl, Ally really, under these stars. I wonder if wishes on plastic stars can still come true.

But the only girl who has ever been in my room is Lizzie and she doesn't really count. She thought the stars were just some sort of bullshit nightlight.

I must fall asleep at some point because the next thing I know, I bolt straight up in bed and hear noise down the hall. Mom and Dad aren't exactly arguing but their voices are tense and loud in the way they get when they're upset, but self-aware enough to know it and trying to be quiet.

My shirt is damp with sweat, so I pull it off. The L-shaped scar that runs around my chest is so ugly I can't stand to look at it. The edges are puckered and red. The doctors say it will fade with time but for now I look like the monster I am.

It's weird to think that somewhere under my skin is Lizzie's heart beating away inside me. Even thinking about it gives me chills so I put my shirt back on and reach my hand under the bed for my baseball mitt.

The leather is warm and smells like summer, freshly

mowed grass, and sweat. It's the one I was going to keep for … it doesn't matter anymore. Still, it feels good to have it on. If I close my eyes and run my hands over the worn laces, I can pretend for a minute that none of this has happened. That the season will start soon and that my biggest decision is going to be whether to play college ball or pray for a minor league contract.

I fall asleep that way. Holding onto the glove like a security blanket. I'm still wearing it when my mom comes in and wakes me up in the middle of the night. I don't think she means to because she's just sitting there, but it's like her thoughts are loud enough to pull me out of whatever thankfully dreamless sleep I've taken refuge in.

"I'm sorry, honey," she says when I open my eyes. "I'm sorry that we didn't know what was going on with Lizzie, and I'm sorry that we didn't tell you what happened."

My mouth opens and then closes. I'm more tired and sad than I am angry at this point. I know she really *is* sorry, but there's nothing I can say.

"When they brought you all into the hospital, everything happened very quickly. Lizzie was a registered organ donor, but because she was a minor they needed her mother's approval," Mom says.

"That nutcase actually agreed to do something nice for someone?" I can't imagine Lizzie's mom approving of anything like that.

Mom gives me a look like she's going to tell me to watch my mouth, but she holds back.

"I think her mother's specific words were that she

didn't care one way or the other." Mom's mouth tightens when she admits this and I'm sure that bit of honesty cost her something. I want to ask if Lizzie's mom was drunk at the time, but as she's pretty much drunk all the time, it's a fair bet she was and it doesn't really matter. Ultimately, it was Lizzie's choice, which is the only thing out of all this craziness that makes me feel a little bit better.

"Spencer knew because he was the one who brought Lizzie's mom to the hospital after he was checked out. There wasn't a lot of time and we didn't want to leave you. Don't be mad at him, honey. He's a good friend."

I smile a little because it's a silly thing for her to be telling me. "No, Mom, it's okay. Spencer and I are fine."

She nods. "Good. And we would have told you, too. It's just that you've been through so much and I can only imagine . . ." She stops and puts her hand on my wrist, the one that still has the mitt on it, and looks at me like she's really seeing me for the first time in forever. "No . . . sorry. I can't really imagine what you're feeling. It's hard sometimes for parents to understand that their kids aren't really kids anymore. But I hope you know that we love you. And that we're here for you."

I choke up a little. This is the most I've heard my mom say in a while that didn't involve notes about keeping my grades up, reminders about changing the oil in the car, or apologies for not making it to my games.

"Thanks," I manage to squeak out.

She gets up to leave and then turns back and takes a card out of her pocket. She looks at it, and then at me, and then back at the card. There's a long pause and then she places it on the nightstand. "Cal, do me one favor. Think about calling Dr. Reynolds. It can't hurt to talk to someone." And then she leaves without waiting for an answer.

I put my glove back under the bed and pick up the card. It's totally official-looking and kind of imposing. Even though I can't imagine why I'd need to talk to anyone other than Spencer about what's going on, I slip it into my mitt so that I'll know where it is. If I need it.

ELEVEN

There's an old maple near the middle school that Spencer, Lizzie, and I carved our names into when we were in seventh grade. Spencer worried that we might damage the tree, but Lizzie was insistent that we do it and, for once, I sided with her against Spencer. I liked the idea of permanence.

We stand in front of it now, me and Spencer, marveling at how much that tree has grown. Even I have to reach up to touch the names we carved with the pocket knife I'd swiped from my dad.

"I never thought we'd end up like this," Spencer says. "I mean, just the two of us."

A breeze picks up and rustles the leaves of the tree, allowing the light to bounce off Spencer's hair. As I watch, the sunshine turns to snow—big, golfball-sized flakes that seem too large to be real.

Spencer leans into me and I can feel his warmth. It's like a fire when you've been freezing, a steak when you've been starving. It fills me until I'm no longer empty.

We stand there, silent, snow falling around our feet until I'm not sure we'll be able to move. Maybe we'll be stuck here next to this old tree for all eternity. I link my arm through Spencer's and the snow starts to fall faster, obscuring my view of everything except the tree and the boy next to me.

"Maybe we shouldn't be here," I say.

Spencer turns to me. He lifts my collar up but leaves his hand, hot, on my neck.

"It doesn't matter where we are, so long as we're together." He leans in, lips parted. His breath is warm enough to melt the snow as it falls, but I shiver anyhow. Shiver hard enough to wake up.

Fucking Lizzie and her dreams.

———————

I try to get back to sleep, but can't get comfortable and just toss and turn. I can't sleep on my stomach or my side like I usually do because of the incision and I've never really liked sleeping on my back. Plus, there's this train that keeps running through my head and the wheels are making that *clack, clack* sound over and over. Lizzie's heart is beating so loudly that it's filling my ears. It gets like this sometimes. Like she wants something, only she's asking for it in a language I can't understand.

Finally I haul myself out of bed and boot up my computer. I'm not sure what to search for. I just feel like there has to be an explanation out there somewhere.

A quick search tells me that the average heart of a seventeen-year-old girl weighs less than a pound.

I type in "organ donation" but get all sorts of legal stuff. Then "Who can donate organs?" but it basically tells me what I already knew, that Lizzie's mom had to agree because Lizzie was under eighteen. I read through all the pages about how normally donated organs would go onto the national registry that Jessica was talking about, so that the organs go to the people who need them most. I guess I understand now why she seemed so pissed at me. Sometimes people have to wait years on the list. Some even die before an organ match is found.

I don't know who would have gotten Lizzie's heart had it not gone to me. And it's strange to think that there might be other bits of her scattered around in other people. Are they feeling her as strongly inside them as I am, or am I the only one hearing her voice because I knew her so well? Or because she knew me?

I click on "directed donation" and find out that it means you give an organ to someone specifically and bypass the registry. Usually this happens when someone gives their sister a kidney or something like that. It doesn't really come into play when someone dies out of the blue. But I guess, in a way, that's what happened to me.

I skip all the parts about survival rates and problems with donated organs being rejected. Somehow I know that my body isn't going to reject Lizzie's heart and not just because I'm being pumped full of drugs to make sure that doesn't happen.

But reading through the information, I'm amazed at all of the ways that things could have gone wrong. Really, the odds of my getting Lizzie's heart were less than the odds of my being hit by lightning. I mean, first of all she had to be there, and be in the correct condition to donate. Then someone had to get her drunken mother there in time and talk her into signing the papers.

And then there are the really hard things. The fact that Lizzie was a tiny bird girl compared to me and that the doctors like the recipient to be the same general size as the donor. And our blood types needed to be the same, which they were. I didn't even know that before.

Next I come across posts about something called cellular memory. It's only a theory really, and I hate theories. But I have to pay attention to this one. It basically says that memories aren't only stored in your brain; they're stored in the cells of your other organs as well.

Like your heart.

So the theory is that when you get someone else's organ, you get their memories. Or at least their likes and dislikes.

Some of the stories I read are funny. There's a guy in Ohio who got a kidney from a girl in Kansas. The girl was some sort of mushroom expert and this guy, who had always hated mushrooms, suddenly wanted them at every meal.

But some of the stories aren't so funny. One is about a guy who got the heart of someone who'd been murdered. And now he was having nightmares about being chased through the woods by a masked killer with a knife.

The articles start to creep me out, so I turn on the rest of the lights in the room, but it really doesn't help. I should shut my computer, but can't look away. Even more, I know Spencer was right. Lizzie would be eating all of this up— she'd totally love it. The freak-out factor would have her researching donated organs for weeks and tormenting me about my loaner heart endlessly.

Something about that idea makes sense, though. Perhaps that's the only way she can still punish me for what I've done to her.

I think it's kind of funny that I don't have any of her tastes. I mean, I haven't suddenly started to listen to old 1960s protest songs and I haven't developed tastes for lacy clothes or rocky road ice cream.

And thankfully, aside from the vague whispers left by her dreams, I don't have any of her memories. I can't imagine having to relive all the crap that went on with her mom. Lizzie was way stronger than I am. I don't know how she put up with all that shit and I'm not sure I could do it. Not even now.

The one thing she hasn't let go of are her feelings for Spencer. I get it. But the dreams are making me crazy. And it isn't like I can just give up sleeping.

Lizzie's voice. *LIZZIE'S VOICE* is like some background noise in my head. What sucks the most is that I have no way of talking to her without feeling like a total idiot. I'd do anything to be able to tell her how sorry I am. I wouldn't even ask her to forgive me because I know that would be impossible. But I'd still want to tell her.

I'm so tired when my alarm goes off that I can barely force my eyes open. I'd love to ditch school today, but then I'd have to explain it to my teachers, and worse, to Spencer and I don't want to be that kid—the one too sick to come to class, the one who needs special considerations.

According to my calendar, the team is having fielding drills today in advance of next week's opening game. Just thinking about it makes my muscles want to make that throw to first. It's funny, I like batting. My average, which now might be frozen like I'm Babe Ruth or some other dead slugger, is .312. I'm one of the team's top hitters in a pretty competitive division, which is rare for a shortstop. But there is something about standing in the field, bent down, waiting for the pitch to be thrown, watching the concentration of the batter and that expectant feeling of waiting for the ball to be hit to me, that I really love. A perfectly turned double play, short-to-second-to-first, is one of the most beautiful things I can think of.

On the field, I'm not afraid of anything. Baseball makes me brave. I trust myself. I trust my teammates. When I'm out there during a game, I don't notice the spectators or anything else. It's just me and the ball and the machine that I form with the rest of the guys.

And now Justin Dillard will be taking my place at short and that thought kills me. It isn't only that I won't be playing, it's that *he* will. He can smack the hell out of a ball even if he can't field one effectively half the time. In fact, his average is only slightly lower than mine. I get that Coach Byrne really has no choice but to play him. That just doesn't make me feel any better.

Ultimately, it's personal.

Earlier this year we were doing these drills where you throw the ball while down on one knee one time, and then from a standing position the next, only you need to keep your body aligned with a stripe on the floor. It would have been fine. Boring, but fine. Except that Dillard kept deliberately throwing the ball slightly off so I had to get up and chase it down through the gym.

"Man, I wouldn't have thought that even you could get this rusty in just a couple of months." Really I should have known better and just kept my mouth shut.

"Well, at least I know what side of the plate I'm batting from," he sneered back at me. I knew his words had nothing to do with baseball.

I remember biting the inside of my cheek to keep from saying anything and whipping the ball at him hard enough that it forced him to take a few steps back. He was the loudest of those who still cared about keeping the gossip about me, Spencer, and Lizzie alive.

What really did it was his next comment.

"Cat got your tongue? Or perhaps you left it in Yeats' mouth."

I was usually able to ignore Dillard's blather. But he pushed it when he mentioned Spencer, and it had been building up inside me for so long that I couldn't just write his words off as the same bullshit he was always spouting.

I landed a hell of a punch before Coach pulled me off him.

He ordered us to the showers and then into his office.

"Which one of you wants to talk first?" Coach asked.

I eyed Dillard suspiciously, curious if there was anything he could say that wouldn't make him look like the ass that he was.

We both stayed silent.

Coach looked back and forth between us. "I'd prefer not to write you both up. I still need one of you to play short. So what do you boys think I should do? Anyone want to give me a reason not to file a report on this?"

I ground my teeth waiting for Dillard to say something stupid, but he just sat there rubbing his jaw, which was starting to swell.

"Sorry, Coach. It won't happen again." I hoped that the fact that I'd never been caught fighting in school before would save me.

Dillard grumbled "sorry" under his breath. What he was sorry for was being caught, not mouthing off to me.

Coach stared at us and sighed. "Get out of my face before I decide to replace both of you. And Dillard, go see the nurse before your face swells up even more. You already look like a chipmunk."

His expression as he walked out meant that he knew I'd won this round.

As I started to leave Coach's office, I heard, "Nice punch, Ryan. I heard what he said. He had it coming. But next time take it outside. Don't you dare do that in my line of sight again, got it?"

Coach kept his head buried in some paperwork, not even looking up.

"Yes sir," I said.

"And Ryan? If there is a next time, make sure it's in the off season. I don't want you busting your hand."

"Yes sir." I hid my smile as I walked out to my next class.

When I ran into Lizzie and Spencer later that day, they'd already heard about the fight. Lizzie called me "slugger" like she was proud of me. Spencer nodded at me once I told him I was okay. But I never told him what had happened to make me deck Dillard.

What I did tell Spencer, and what I remember now and pretty much every time I think of throwing that punch, is this: "It felt really, really good."

I take a super-hot shower and my meds, but still must look tired because my mom gives me one of her looks as I get ready to leave. She goes so far as to put the back of her hand on my forehead, checking to see if I have a fever and I have to push her off.

The only good thing about the morning is that when Spencer picks me up, it's with a large cup of decaf coffee. It may not be "real" coffee, but at least I can pretend that I'm drinking something that will wake me up.

Of course he also greets me with, "Man, you look like crap."

"You always know what to say to make me feel good, Yeats," I joke as I slide into Sweeney and gulp down the coffee.

"No, seriously, you're okay, right?" he asks, and honestly, even though he means well, I'm so sick of that question I could scream.

"Let's make a deal. You won't ask that again and I promise that you'll be the first person I tell if I'm not."

Spencer smiles apologetically. "Sorry. It's a deal."

There's a silence in the car that's waiting to be broken, a heavy cloud above me that's made it impossible to have a normal conversation about anything. Even more, there are ghosts of conversations that hang between me and Spencer. It's still eating at me that he and Lizzie slept together. It isn't jealousy; it's some odd twisted anger I don't understand. And our conversation yesterday about my having Lizzie's heart feels like it's demanding to be discussed. But I don't want to talk about it. I don't want to talk about hearts. I don't want to even think about how much I hate myself for what I did to Lizzie, and I certainly don't want to talk about how Lizzie's dreams of him are still invading my nights. So when I break the silence it's to ask about Spencer's kinda-sorta-boyfriend in Seattle. "So what's up with Rob?"

"What's up with Ally?" he lobs back.

"Come on, that isn't fair. You guys are at least actually friends. I mean, you email him and everything." And what I mean by that is that he doesn't turn into a total idiot every time he even thinks of talking to Rob, like I do with Ally.

"It isn't that hard. All you need to do is say hello to her," Spencer says in that way he has of boiling things down and making them sound easier than they are.

"I've said hello," I say, fiddling with the strap of my backpack.

Spencer rolls his eyes at me and smiles, but like all of his smiles lately it's forced and almost empty. "Yeah, and then you need to say something else."

I flip the buckle of the seat belt open and closed, open and closed. If someone hits the car now there would be a fifty percent chance of my being protected by the belt depending on the timing. "That's where I get stuck."

"You should have let Lizzie talk to Ally for you when she wanted to."

I have no idea whether he's kidding or not. My breath catches a little bit anyhow. The idea of Lizzie being the one to approach Ally on my behalf was one of the most terrifying things I'd ever heard. It took weeks of begging and pleading on my part to get her to promise that she wouldn't say anything to Ally. Even then I was looking over my shoulder all the time because Lizzie wouldn't have been subtle, and she wouldn't have been vague, and I would have been mortified.

But now, if she were here, I'd almost let her. It would almost be worth whatever embarrassment came from it to have her here screwing with my life again.

"It wouldn't have ended well," I say.

Spencer laughs a little. "Oh absolutely not. But it would have started a conversation and you need to talk to her. To Ally."

My talking to Ally was a pipe dream before the accident. On one hand, I probably have nothing left to lose and should go for broke. On the other, it might make more sense for me to concentrate on keeping my grades together and figuring out what the hell kind of a future I have now that I can't play ball.

I don't know how to explain to Spencer, confident Spencer, who can say anything to anyone and make it sound interesting and convincing, that any chance I ever had with Ally is probably gone. I can't tell him how not being able to play baseball makes me feel like I don't even know who I am anymore. Lizzie's dreams aren't making that easier either. How much can I lose before I lose myself? Or who I thought I was?

There's no way I can throw that question at Spencer without him thinking that I'm nuts, so I make some noncommittal noise that he realizes is a noncommittal noise. Once again, he's managed to resist talking about Rob and I've managed to resist talking about Ally and we've both managed to avoid talking about Lizzie. We both know that all those conversations might be tabled, but none of them are really over.

TWELVE

After a couple of days of school, I get back into the rhythm of things. Government follows English follows Chem. My brain falls back into these patterns the same way I used to be able to step up to the plate on the first day of spring training and fall into my swing from muscle memory.

The familiarity of taking the same classes and sitting in the same seats day after day after day actually helps more than I could have guessed. And now that everyone has pretty much stopped pointing and staring at me, I can zone out and lose myself in things I don't care about, like *Wuthering Heights*, and things I do care about, like how thunderstorms develop into tornados.

Aside from the fact that I really need to start focusing on my grades to get me through to college, classes take my mind off Lizzie, and my guilt, and the gray cloud of sadness that follows me around more often than not. Lizzie pretty much hated school. She's tuned out during the day so my head is totally mine.

"Dude. Really?" Ben leans over my arm while we're waiting for class to start. At first I have no idea what he's talking about, but then I follow his eyes down to my notebook. I slam it shut as fast as I can on what would have been a nude drawing of Spencer Yeats.

"Prank," I say although I know he's not going to believe me. Today it's Spencer, yesterday it was a mound of skulls. Flowers were growing out of the eyes of one. Snakes slithered through another. One looked suspiciously like Assistant Principal Stiller.

I've never been able to draw. I almost flunked my distributional art class. But apparently I've gotten over it.

"Damn it, Lizzie. Stop," I mutter under my breath. Thankfully, we have a sub today. Everyone is having their own conversations, so no one except Ben is looking at the crazy boy talking to himself in the corner and even he's moved his chair noticeably farther away from me.

I sit with my hands linked together for the rest of the day, only picking up a pen when I need to take some notes and hoping that Ben will forget what he thought he saw or at least that he stays quiet about it.

As usual, though, things get worse when class is over. In the time that used to be filled with baseball and with Lizzie—the whole Lizzie, not just her voice—I'm lost. Somehow, I have too much time on my hands and not enough. I'm lonely, but at the same time I feel like I can't get a minute alone.

With nothing else to occupy my thoughts, Lizzie is everywhere. She's in my head. Coursing through my veins. She takes over to the point that there are evenings when I wonder if any of the things I'm thinking are really mine.

I'm using my study hall hours to work out in the gym like Dr. Collins suggested. The school has been great about allowing it. But come four o'clock on days when Spencer is in rehearsal and Lizzie is just a voice inside my head, the thought of going home and being alone makes my skin crawl.

So I've developed this kind of route that takes me around the school. I hang out in the library talking to Mrs. Finn, the librarian, about new books that have come in that I'll probably never read. I hover in the music rooms to listen to the choir practice and watch the marching band go through its drills. Today, I head to the auditorium to sit in on part of Spencer's rehearsal.

I'm almost to the door when I see her. Ally. Leaning against the wall, dressed in white for the show, and holding a sword. She looks like some fierce angel and I don't really realize it until I see her, but I've been avoiding her since I came back to school.

I imagine walking up to her, asking her to dance with me in the halls or run outside to play in the rain. For one minute it doesn't matter that I have this scar and these medications like some old man. For a minute I'm going to take charge.

Just do it already.

"God, Lizzie …" The words escape my mouth before I can stop them and my stomach clenches with worry. Hearing her voice is one thing. Talking back to it in front of other people is another kind of crazy and it's starting to become a bad habit.

When I look back at Ally, she catches my eye. It makes me so flustered that I walk right by her. Spencer would kill me if he knew I'd chickened out. Lizzie would have been giving me a crazy hard time as well. I will the voice in my head to stay quiet just this once.

But then I stop again. For a minute I picture myself turning around and going back. Talking to her. Just saying something. Anything to break this stupid stalemate.

Then, as I'm about to turn, I hear a voice behind me. "Hey, sweet cheeks." It's Justin Dillard, and I know he isn't talking to me.

I'm halfway inside the door. In front of me, ribbons of fabric unfurl from the top of the stage. I turn my head and crane my neck back to see Ally offer Dillard a tired smile.

"Hey, Justin." Just hearing her say his name makes me want to hit something.

I wonder if they're dating, wonder if the entire world has gone crazy while I've been gone.

In the space of time it takes him to answer, I ride a roller-coaster ride of emotions: anger at him for being such a jerk, disgust at myself for even thinking I'd have a chance with her, fury at the universe for not letting me catch a break, and a sadness so deep and acidic that it feels like I'm burning up from the inside.

His response, "I want to talk about prom," propels me away from them and down the stairs.

I'm gasping for air, feel like I'm going to throw up.

Before I know it, I'm in The Cave. It's the first time I've been here since the night of Lizzie's birthday and it feels like our laughter from that night is trapped in the black of the walls, mocking me. I can hear our voices in my mind. Not like the ones that sound like Lizzie is whispering straight into my ear. These are more like an old scratchy record that's stuck in a groove on repeat.

It's freezing and dark. Spencer isn't here so there are no candles lit and I feel more alone than I ever have. Even with Lizzie inside me.

Then I remember the ghost.

"Alice, are you here?" I ask the air. It's stupid, but if I can feel Lizzie inside me shouldn't I be able to contact this poor girl whose spirit is supposed to be here somewhere?

I don't know what I'm expecting. Like maybe all of a sudden I'm some ghost whisperer? I keep calling her name louder and louder, but there's no answer. Even the damned ghost doesn't want anything to do with me. Even she knows who I am: someone who kills their friends. Someone who has nothing left.

I don't notice the door opening and the recessed lighting coming on until suddenly, it's light and Spencer is there with his arm around me.

"It's okay. It's all going to be okay," he murmurs.

For the first time, Spencer's reassurances sound false. Maybe he actually believes that things are going to be fine because for Spencer they always are. But I'm starting to think he needs to understand that the rest of the world isn't so lucky.

"I saw you in the doorway at rehearsal. Why didn't you come in?" he asks when I don't reply.

I pull away. I can't stand still. My mind is reeling with regret. After over a year I was almost considering *doing* something instead of hanging back like a scared little kid. I was seconds away from talking to Ally instead of just sitting back, but as usual I waited too long and now I'm screwed.

"Ally. Are she and Justin together?" My words come out breathy like I've been running sprints.

He shrugs. It's obvious he has no idea what has me so worked up. "What? I don't think so. I've seen him hanging around, but he doesn't exactly seem like her type."

My thoughts are cycling, jumping from one horrible thought to another and I'm not sure which one to address first.

"Why don't they lock me up?" I ask him. After all, that's what they do with people who kill their friends. I don't get it. Do they think I'm going to die so it won't matter anyhow?"

Now Spencer looks completely confused. "For what?"

"God, Spencer, I killed Lizzie. I could have killed you too."

Spencer shakes his head like he can't believe I've brought it up again. His voice is almost a monotone as he repeats the mantra I've heard from him over and over since the accident. "You didn't kill anybody. That driver … "

"Wasn't paying attention. I get it," I scream at him. My voice bounces off the walls and I'm surprised at how good it feels to yell, and to not care if I'm being nice or saying what I'm supposed to say. "Everybody needs to stop fucking using that as some sort of excuse. We could have left five minutes later. I could have insisted that she put her seat belt back on. I could have let you drive." I'm spinning out of control, but I can't seem to stop. This anger, this explosive rage, isn't Lizzie either. It's all me.

Spencer grabs me by the arms and his face is something I'm not sure I've ever really seen, not even onstage. He's seriously angry. I can only hope that he's angry at me because he finally understands that this is all my fault; but really, I'm not sure what he's thinking.

"Do you think I'm lying to you?" he hisses.

"What?" I yank my arm and try to pull out of his grasp but he's stronger than I've given him credit for and he doesn't let go.

"Do you think I'm just saying all of this to make you feel better? I mean, because it was just some girl who died, right? Someone who didn't matter to me at all?"

His anger, his sarcasm, shocks the hell out of me because it's so unlike him. I feel like one of those bullets that shatter into a million pieces when it hits a target, only Spencer is the closest thing to me and he keeps getting hit with the shrapnel. Whatever guilt I'm already wrestling with boils over and I can feel hot tears burst out from some dam inside me and come streaming down my face.

Rain delay.

Lizzie is still such a smart-ass. But her words force me to take a breath.

"Yeats, I didn't mean it like that. I just ... I should have done something, you know? It should have been me," I say. This time I do pull away and smack the nearest one of those damned cubes as hard as I can. I barely feel it. My jumbled emotions are too strong for me to pay attention to anything else.

"Don't do that, Cal. Don't you dare do that," Spencer says from across the room. He and I have never fought about anything. This is uncharted territory for us and I don't like it.

"Do what?" I swipe at the tears that keep falling down my face.

"Say that it should have been you. I've already lost one best friend; I can't lose you, too. There was nothing…" Now that he's stalked over to me, I can see tears hanging in the corner of his eyes too. "There was nothing you could have done." He takes a deep breath and then admits, "I know that you've had other things on your mind. I know this all sucks, but it's hard for me too. To know that a part of her is inside you. It's like I'm talking to both of you at once."

His words hit me like a hundred-mile-an-hour fastball to the chest. They push me back until I'm sitting and for a second I can't breathe. Not once with everything that's gone on have I really stopped to think about how this was affecting him. I thought about Lizzie. I thought about myself. Hell, I even thought about how this would affect the team. But not once did I give any thought to how it would affect my best friend to have lost Lizzie, who was one of his best friends, who he *slept with*, and to have her heart inside me.

"Fuck, Yeats. I'm sorry, I'm sorry," I say over and over. I can't seem to find any other words, but I've offered too many apologies for any of them to carry any weight. I rest my head in my hands and wish that I could disappear or turn back the clock.

Spencer sighs and sits down on the cube next to me. His shoulder presses against mine and I can feel him pulling himself together before he starts to talk again. "You know…Lizzie and I…" he begins and I know what he's about to say. For a second I think about letting him wrestle with the words and have to say them. It would serve him right and the part of me deep inside that is Lizzie wants him to have to articulate it, but ultimately, the part that is me can't stand the look of loss that crosses his face.

"I know," I blurt out, wondering why it seemed so important to both of them to confess to me, when neither of them said anything at the time. "She told me."

He looks surprised, but nods as if he's thinking, "Of course she did. How could I have thought otherwise?"

"She didn't tell me any details, not even about when it happened." I'm fishing and I know that it isn't any of my business and I'm not even sure why I care. What difference does it really make anymore? But of course Spencer can hear the curiosity in my voice.

"It was after the *Bacchus* cast party right before Thanksgiving. Remember she came with you, but you had a test the next day and left early so I said I'd drive her home?"

I do remember that night. And so does Lizzie because I feel … something … pulse inside me as he speaks.

"I hate closing nights," Spencer continues, but I know this. The only time he ever seems depressed and down is after a show ends. And I get it. It's pretty much how I've always felt at the end of a baseball season. "But I was really wired that night for some reason. And Lizzie was in rare form. I don't think I stopped laughing the whole time."

We both sit there wrapped in our own memories of Lizzie and my brain is buzzing like I just had a six pack of cola injected into my veins.

Then Spencer sighs again. "Her mom and the loser were both out when I got her home and took her up to her room. Simon spiked the punch and she'd had a bit. She wasn't drunk or anything, I just wanted to make sure that she fell asleep upstairs and away from them, you know? That she remembered to lock the door behind her.

"She was wearing one of those lacy dresses that she loved and the window was open and the full moon was shining in and through the fabric. It framed her like she was backlit. And we were happy and laughing. It had been a really, really good night. It made me feel good to see her that relaxed. She was so ethereal in that moment."

I look at him and his unshed tears are making his eyes shine in the dim light. But he doesn't look sad, he looks wistful. Not at all like he's confessing something that he regrets or is embarrassed by.

Then he laughs a little. "It was kind of a perfect storm of Lizzie."

So that's what it was, I hear in my head.

Honestly, I know what he's talking about because as harsh and rough around the edges as she could be, Lizzie was also beautiful in a willowy, damaged type of way that we were each attracted to for our own reasons, and in our own ways.

"And then ... honestly, I don't even know which of us started it. One minute we were just standing there and the next ... it just kind of happened," he says and blushes. "It felt really, really right at the time."

He looks up at me like a puppy dropping a ball at its owner's feet and looking for approval.

"But you're gay," I say stupidly and instantly regret it.

Spencer cocks his head and stares at me like I've lost my mind for stating something so obvious, because ever since we were eleven and he forced me to watch his dad's DVD of some British production of *Hamlet* from the '80s, it's been clear that it was Hamlet who got him worked up and not Ophelia.

"Sorry," I squeak out.

"Look, I don't expect you to understand. I'm not even sure that I do. Not really. But it was just Lizzie and I love her." He stops and a million things cross his face at once. "Loved her. Love her. *Fuck*. It just wasn't..."

"Yeah, I know," I chime in. Neither Lizzie nor I need to hear this explanation. I can feel her reacting, though. I'm not hearing her voice, but there is something... feelings that are rushing through me that aren't mine. Love. Lust. Frustration. A whole lot of frustration. Remembering.

It isn't like the scene is playing in front of me, movie-like. Instead it's in the back of my head clicking through reel-by-reel like an old film, one that I can't really watch but I can feel as the emotions fly through it.

I blink my eyes, but that doesn't make it go away. I'm glad that they had their moment but I don't really want to share it. I just want to make the buzzing stop and get Lizzie's desperate yearning for Spencer out of me. It's like a weight that's pulling me down to someplace I don't think I can visit.

I kind of get that Spencer is telling me all this because it's important to him. And I get that he needs to tell me this story and that, while maybe I didn't need to hear it before, I do now. I need to make it okay for him. He needs Lizzie to... I don't know. I can't sort that part out. Forgive him? I'm not sure how to ask him. Or if he even knows the answer.

There are questions swirling through my head that Lizzie wants answers to, but those are ones I refuse to ask. She had her chance and there are places I simply won't go. Places I won't ask him to go.

I want her to back off, but I know that isn't going to happen. This is the strongest I've felt her since the accident. My skin feels like I'm in an electric storm—all the hair on my arms is standing straight up. I have to do something—and quickly—to change the course of the conversation and I know just how to do it.

"Don't take this the wrong way, but..." I start and then stop. The time is finally right to confront Spencer about what's been bothering me ever since Lizzie first told me about them being together. I'm not as bugged out as I used to be, but it still feels like something that needs to be said.

"You don't think it was kind of stupid and selfish or anything, do you?"

"What?" Spencer's eyes narrow and I have to look away before I can continue.

"Come on, Yeats, really? What planet were you on when you thought that having sex with Lizzie was a good idea?" I feel a sharp jab deep inside my head, like an ice pick is trying to bore its way out.

"It wasn't like I planned it ahead of time," he says sadly.

"Yeah? Well maybe you should have."

Suddenly I'm owning this anger that I've tried to hold in. My head feels like it's going to split in two.

"I..." For once Spencer Yeats is speechless and I feel like a dick for being the one to make him that way.

"You knew how she felt about you," I say, realizing that I said almost the same thing to Lizzie.

"I know," he says and his voice cracks. It's a defeated

sound, one I've never heard from him. "I didn't do it to hurt her. I mean, it wasn't about the sex. And she was the one who ... I just didn't stop her."

His voice echoes inside my head. And then: *Cal Ryan, I swear to God that if you make Spencer feel bad about sleeping with me I will haunt your every fucking thought for the rest of your life.*

Because I have no doubt that she means it, and because hurting Spencer really is the last thing I want to do, I force, "I'm sorry" out of my lips. Again.

Spencer runs his hands through his mop of hair, which springs back into place automatically. "I miss her so much," he says, and it's only the tip of the iceberg.

Lizzie's heart skips a beat and for a minute I wonder if I'm going to have to call 911, but no, it's just her, I guess. "She knows that." I bite my cheek, afraid that I've given too much away. Thankfully Spencer is too distracted to notice.

"I wish ... " he starts and it rips me up inside to see the pain that crosses his face. I've known Spencer for so many years that sometimes looking at him is like looking at myself in the mirror. I know every expression and what it means and whether it's really him or a role he's thrown himself into even for just a sentence.

But that means the pain on his face is real and it's killing me, shredding me inside. I want to take that pain away but I don't know how.

"I wish ... " he starts again and I'm praying in my head that he finishes the sentence because I want to know what he wants and what I can do. Inside me Lizzie's heart beats too hard, like she's waiting as well. Both of us are waiting to know the same thing: how do we make it better for him?

"I wish it would have been different," he says. "I wish I could have loved her the way she wanted. The way that she needed me to. Maybe I should have tried harder."

"Spence," I say, reaching out to grab his arm. And then I stop. And he looks at me because I've never called him Spence. That was Lizzie's name for him. "Yeats," I say, but I'm backtracking and it's too late. I'm not really in control of what's happening. Of my mind. Of my body. Lizzie has always been stronger-willed than me and now less than a pound of her inside me is calling the shots. And even though I've done my best to keep him in the dark, I can see something in Spencer's eyes that makes me think he knows Lizzie is here. That he's speaking to her more than he is to me.

But I keep talking anyhow because staying silent is like admitting something I'm not ready to confess. "That's ridiculous. You don't just choose things like that. Besides, I don't think she cared," I say and mean it. "I mean … she was happy to have whatever part of you she could."

He stands and I can see a hint of his mega-watt smile tinged with deep, deep sadness. "She said that to me, you know. After. Maybe it should have made me feel better, but it actually made me feel worse."

"Why?"

"Because she really did love me that much. Or maybe because I loved her that much too." He runs his hand through his hair again as I watch him try to sort out the words he's looking for. "I wanted to stay there with her.

In her bed. I wanted to stop and pretend it could really be that easy. That Lizzie and I were on a desert island somewhere and that her mom wasn't going to be coming home from the bar half-smashed. And that I wasn't... I mean, maybe, we could be together. Really together. Maybe that was all she really needed to turn things around."

He takes a deep breath and I let him continue, his words tripping over themselves while I get up and lean against a stack of the cubes and knot my hands together to try to keep my warring emotions, Lizzie's emotions, contained.

"When I kissed her the last time it physically hurt me to walk away. It's the only time..." Thankfully, he doesn't finish his sentence because I'm not sure I can stand to hear the rest of it. "Anyhow, as I walked out of her room she said 'thank you' like I'd given her some gift or something. I almost turned around and went back to her. I fought with myself to leave. I'm still not sure if it was the right choice or not."

Something rages through me like a fire out of control. It's the first thing besides anger to really reach me since the accident. I don't know what it is, but it's intense in a way that feels like it will kill me if I don't give into it. I'm literally drowning in Lizzie's emotions and I feel so weak and tired and confused by what to do to help the two people I love most, that for a heartbeat I just give in. And the .857th of a second that it takes for her heart to beat is enough for Lizzie, who has probably been waiting for this chance ever since the accident.

She raises my hands slowly, so slowly, like they're moving towards a wild animal but it's only Spencer and whatever else happens I know that he isn't going to hurt either of us in any way.

Inside, though, I'm shaking. I'm not sure if I should be trying to fight her or not. I'm dizzy and terrified of the feelings and electric jolts that are running through me.

I watch as my hands loop around Spencer's neck and pull him close to me and we're eye-to-eye. He doesn't look scared or even curious. He looks like he always does, like everything is okay and like everything will be okay. And I want to believe that. I need to believe that.

I stand there waiting even though Lizzie wants to rush ahead. I still have a shred of control over things, but I'm stuck in time. I'm not helping her, not fighting her. My sheer terror has frozen all of my muscles and I feel like I did when I was in the hospital with that damned tube down my throat and no way to communicate.

I expect Spencer to say something. To pull back. To crack a joke. But he doesn't. I can see the calm lifting and falling of his chest as he breathes normally. He raises his arms and puts them around my waist. They feel strong and I can smell the familiar scent of the ridiculously expensive English shaving cream he insists on using.

It feels like years go by as we stand like that. It feels like there's time to choose what path this is going to take. Tentacles of possibilities snaking out in every different direction. But there is only one thing that Lizzie wants and she isn't going to be detoured. And I wonder if maybe I owe her this. She'll never grow up, never fall in love with anyone else, hell, she'll never have sex again. She'll never have the time to get her life sorted out and create more amazing paintings and get away from her awful family and pull it all together. And regardless of what anyone else says, it's my fault. I was driving. I should have been able to save her. Instead she saved me and now I think that I owe her this one minute in time.

Lizzie's heart is pounding like it's going to jump out of my chest and I wonder how long my body can take it. I wonder if waiting, standing stuck here like this is going to kill me, kill Lizzie again and it is that thought that propels me forward. But it is one sharp tremor that makes me lose control.

Cal's body moves forward slightly and Spence closes his eyes but I don't close Cal's. I want this. I don't want to miss a minute of it. I want to see his face, the beautiful face that I'm reaching out and touching with hands that aren't mine.

I hesitate slightly because sometimes the wanting is as good as the having. I learned that when I was alive and spent a lot of time wanting things I was never going to get, such as Spence, and a future, and normal parents who gave a damn.

And then Spence tilts his head and pulls Cal towards him. His lips are as soft as I remember and I feel fire surge through me, through Cal, through Spence. His tongue explores Cal's mouth and I almost want to cry because it feels so good, and right, and complete. It's the only time I've ever understood Cal's comments about perfect moments and stopping time. I would stop time and damn the whole screwed-up world to keep this kiss going.

Somewhere in the distance, I can feel Cal analyzing this

like he analyzes everything. He loves Spence, but he is such a damned guy *and thinks it's fine for Spence to be gay, but that he can't possibly allow himself to enjoy this. He isn't sure what he feels and he hates that.*

But I know what I feel and I take charge. I exhale slightly and then inhale Spence's air and for a moment, I think that even when we were having sex we weren't this close. Perhaps it's as simple as Spence missing me and understanding that this is the end. Or perhaps it's because this is Cal's body, athletic and toned even after all of the time in the hospital and undeniably male, but that's okay. I don't mind. We don't get to choose who we're attracted to or who we love. They say "the heart wants what the heart wants" and the appropriateness of that would make me laugh, would make all of us laugh, if I didn't think saying it would ruin the moment. Because really, isn't that exactly what's going on?

I want to focus on this kiss, and the next and the next because Spence isn't stopping. His hands are in Cal's hair and even though I only feel it like an echo, I can feel Cal's response like ripples of thunder are rolling through him. And that is wonderful enough.

I push forward, running my hands, Cal's hands, under Spence's shirt and the feel of his skin makes me feel like I'm drunk and the room begins to spin. Spence's breath is coming in short gasps that are pulling me in deeper and deeper. I want to make him want me. Really want me until he can't hold back any more.

I want to keep going, to keep pushing, to see how far Spence will let me go, but at the same time I know that this is going to end somewhere. Suddenly I wish it wasn't Cal's body that was housing my heart. Because that means I'll have to stop before we get into territory that will seriously fuck Cal up, no pun intended. As it is, I can tell he's barely holding it together.

I wish I didn't give a shit about Cal, but I do. I care about him as much as I care about Spence, and caring about someone that much makes you responsible for them in a way. And I finally realize why they were always there when I needed them. They felt responsible not because I was the world's biggest train wreck, but just because, improbable as it might have been, they loved me.

I pull back slightly. Cal inhales and his eyes are closed now because I don't want to see if Spence is looking at him in horror or with something closer to the look he gave me when we were up in my room that night. That pure and almost ridiculously loving look that no one else has ever given me. It's that look I'm dying to see again, but terrified of at the same time because I've spent too many years convincing myself that I was unlovable and that's made dying easier.

But I can't help it, this not knowing, or perhaps that's Cal who can't help it and his eyes open. Spence looks . . . angelic and perfect. The white shirt under his gray sweater is bringing out the blue in his eyes, which are literally sparkling. They say that people's eyes sparkle, but I've never seen eyes actually light up like Spence's, like they're reflecting fireworks going on inside him. And he's looking through Cal to me.

"Liz?" he asks, looking both sad and amazed.

I nod. I want to reply. I want to tell him so much, but I can't make Cal's voice work and while he isn't fighting me, he isn't helping much.

I pull back slightly and Cal opens his mouth.

"She's ... " I say and then can't say anything else. I'm feeling too much, none of which I understand and I'm more than happy to crawl back away inside my mind and let Lizzie have control over my body, only that isn't really how it is. Like it or not, I'm still here with her.

Lizzie doesn't want this to stop. And for once, I have no idea what Spencer wants. Or perhaps that's a lie. Perhaps I do and just don't have a damned clue how to deal with it.

Either way, Spencer nods and leans towards me, his breath warm on my neck. My vision narrows, making me feel like I'm falling down a long dark tunnel. And it would scare the hell out of me if it weren't for Spencer, his hands on my arms, holding me here, making it okay.

THIRTEEN

Some mornings you wake up and it's like the skies part and everything gets clear and sunny and suddenly makes sense.

This isn't one of those mornings.

My head is pounding, my scars are itching like crazy, and my lips ... holy crap, my lips feel raw and bruised. Just to make it worse, Dr. Collins is expecting me for my weekly appointment and he isn't going to care how fractured and screwed up I'm feeling.

Right now I want something I usually don't. I want to be alone. I want to sink into silence and try to make sense of what happened last night. But of course I'm not alone. I'm not sure I'm ever going to be alone again. And Lizzie is shooting bursts of adrenaline-fueled joy through me. She won't even back off and let me be tormented by the fact that I made out with my best friend.

I keep telling myself that she isn't deliberately trying to torture me. She's wired and manic. No change from how she always was where Spencer was concerned. Only now I'm stuck in the middle in a way I never was before and really, I want no part of it.

I can't outrun Lizzie, but I'm trying to avoid everyone else. I've already convinced Mom to let me use her car. It doesn't make sense for her to drive me to the hospital and sit there while they're running all of their tests. Plus I miss the sense of freedom that comes with driving. I had to promise to call her when I get there. I had to promise to take all side roads. I had to basically beg and plead like a little kid before she gave in.

But now that I'm in the car, I just sit here. My brain knows what it's meant to do: put my seat belt on, adjust my mirrors, put the key in the ignition, turn it, take the car out of park, drive. But my body is rebelling. Tense. Shaking. Sweat is already pouring down the back of my neck, soaking the collar of my shirt.

It's just driving. I've done it a thousand times, but my hands can't seem to get the seat belt into the little metal slot. I hear Spencer's voice in my head telling me to breathe, to take one thing at a time, that everything will be okay. I'm happy and surprised to find that, even after last night, thinking of him helps some. At least enough that I can get the seat belt on, the mirrors moved, and the key in the ignition.

I turn on the radio and am assaulted by classical music because this is, after all, my mom's car and she likes to listen to classical on her way to court. I reach over to change it, but can't imagine what I would want to hear. My already-pounding head can't deal with the thought of my usual rock stations. Sports channels are going to depress me and make me remember everything I've lost. There's classic rock, but that will make me think of Lizzie and all the other things I've lost.

I turn the radio off, but I never drive without music so the silence actually makes me even more uncomfortable. I flip it back to classical, turn it down, and put my hand on the gear shift while I stare at the letters P and D. Only inches make up the difference between sitting here, safe in my parents' driveway, and actually moving, driving, controlling this metallic monster that can get me from point A to point B.

I used to think of a car as being a means to an end: a moving house that took me from one place to another. Now it's something new. Now it's a loaded gun in my hand.

————————

"Seriously, I don't mind," Spencer says, hands on the wheel of his car. He looks like he's about to go onstage; all ironed and pulled together. In fact, he looks so relaxed it makes me wonder if I imagined everything last night.

But I know better, and the way Lizzie's heart is galloping in my chest isn't leaving any room for doubt. I slink down in the passenger's seat. "Can we not talk about it?"

He looks in the rear-view mirror and backs us down the drive. "How many times have you driven me to school or home from rehearsal? Just think of it as my evening up the score."

"Thanks. Really. I just need to get a handle on things." After I say it, I realize how many ways my comment can be taken, and I'm praying that he knows that I'm talking about driving and not about anything that may or may not have happened in The Cave.

If I'm embarrassed about having to ask him to drive me to my appointment then I'm mortified about whatever the hell it was that happened after school. This morning is the first time that I've ever hesitated to call Spencer about anything. And I know it wasn't because my parents had already left and I didn't want to impose on him for a ride, or because my hands were shaking so hard I thought I was going to drop the phone.

"If it'll help, we can go to the mall after your appointment and you can putter around the lot there and get used to driving again. I'm free until rehearsal at three," Spencer offers.

It's an offer that means a lot. Spencer never lets anyone drive Sweeney, so I nod and try to focus on what should be a simple thought: driving. Driving with him in the car, wondering if that would be easier or if I'd just be afraid of hurting him too. Wondering if I can really sit in a car with him and not think about yesterday. About our lips...and his hands...

I feel hot and cold and dizzy like I'm going to be sick. I'm tired from fighting like hell against Lizzie wanting to replay, again and again, that half hour in The Cave that felt like it lasted for a year. Against her wanting to remember how easy it was to fall into his arms and feel safe, and at the same time buzzing like, for the first time, I was aware of nerve endings I never knew I had.

I look down to see that my hands are clutching at the armrest and that I'm sitting so far over, there's almost room for another person between us in the front seat of Spencer's little Golf.

Spencer must notice it too because when I look up, he catches my eye. "Look, about last night..." he starts quietly.

I put my hands over my eyes and rub them, trying to wipe the memories out of my head. I glance at the speedometer and try to calculate whether I'd survive jumping out of the moving car. It seems unlikely. My luck isn't exactly good these days. "I'm sorry," I whisper, keeping my eyes straight ahead. "I'm just…"

The words get stuck in my throat, choking me to the point that I can barely breathe. I roll down the window and try to gulp in as much air as my lungs can hold.

All I hear is the deafening sound of blood rushing through my head and the hum of the engine as we lurch over to the side of the road. I'd almost welcome a meeting with the guardrail.

Spencer pulls down a side street and it takes him a minute to turn the ignition off, but then he does and pulls his leg up onto the seat, twisting so that he's facing me.

"Okay, so I get why you bolted last night. I really do," he says. He blushes slightly and fiddles with his shoelaces. My stomach twists.

"Yeats…" I begin, even though I have nothing at all to say, which Spencer must know because he just barrels on.

"I tried to call you last night. A couple of times."

I nod. I ended up hiding my phone under a pile of dirty clothes. The light of the screen cast eerie shadows through my blue T-shirt every time it went off. I still haven't listened to the messages. I knew they'd make me feel worse.

I can't even look at him now, although I feel his eyes lying heavy on me.

"I didn't want things to get like this between us," he says. "Awkward."

I nod again and look out the window desperate for a star

to wish on. I'd wish for this to all be over. I'd wish for us to be like we've always been and to forget this ever happened. But it's morning and it's fitting that all I can see are clouds.

Spencer reaches out and tugs on my sleeve. "Are you okay?"

I force myself to look at him and the concern on his face makes me feel worse. I *want* to be okay. I think about what he said in The Cave about having already lost Lizzie and about not wanting to lose me too. I don't want to take another friend away from him. I'm tired and confused and this whole thing sucks, but the one thing I know for sure, the only thing that I don't have to question, is that losing Spencer would completely kill me.

I shrug. I know I should say something; I just can't bring my mouth to move.

"Cal, we've been best friends forever and I don't want anything to mess that up. I probably should have stopped things. I mean, you took me by surprise, but that's no excuse. I know how screwed up things have been for you lately. How screwed up they'd have to be for you to ... "

A low groan escapes my lips. I'd give almost anything not to have to talk about this. Spencer, on the other hand, is on a roll.

"And I should probably feel guilty for not really being sorry it happened. I mean, I admit for a long time I kind of used to wonder ... "

My head snaps back hard against the window. "You used to wonder what?" I ask, trying to figure out what the hell that combination of words mean.

A heavy silence hangs in the car. "Yeah. Okay." He breathes out the words in a resigned puff of air, pushing up the sleeves of his shirt like he's getting ready to go into battle. "What do want me to say, Cal? I mean, we've been best friends longer than I've even been sure I was gay. And it isn't like you're an ogre or anything, quite the opposite."

My mouth is hanging open and I'm pretty sure I'm staring at Spencer like he's an alien who was accidently beamed into the car. I can't think of a single word to say in response to his confession.

Spencer leans forward and links his hands around his bent knee. "I know you're freaked out and I'm truly sorry for that. I really am. You have to believe me. But I'm not going to lie and say that it was horrible, because it wasn't. In fact, it was actually..." Now he's grinning and I'm pretty sure he only stops because if I look as green as I'm feeling, he's worried about my puking on Sweeney's sparkling-clean upholstery.

I swallow so loudly I'm sure he can hear it, and then say "fine," which I know means nothing when your best friend has just told you he didn't mind you and the girl living in your body—your heart—mauling him in the school theater.

A small smile holds up one side of his mouth. Nothing ever seems to embarrass him for long, which, I guess, is something I've always envied about Spencer Yeats. I can't ever hope to be that comfortable in my own skin.

My head is buzzing like a box of bees. My feelings and Lizzie's are so jumbled that I can't really tell them apart. Just like yesterday.

"Lizzie." I stop and take a few deep breaths. I mean, if Spencer can tell me all this stuff, then maybe, just maybe I can too and he won't think I'm nuts. Maybe. Or maybe it would be worse.

A shadow crosses his face. He reaches up and plays with the air conditioner, readjusting the vents until I have to force my hands under my legs to resist the urge to stop him.

"What's it like?" he finally asks.

"What's what like?"

"Having part of Lizzie inside you like that? I mean, for a minute it was like she was there or something." He gives me a sheepish smile. "You probably think I'm unhinged for even saying that, right?"

"Yeah, totally off your rocker. It's not her, just a mess of tissue. Just veins, muscle, and blood," I mumble. I feel like a traitor to Lizzie for saying it and I'm not sure why she isn't yelling at me in my head; why she's been so quiet through this whole ridiculous conversation.

Spencer folds his arms tight against his chest like he's ready to defend her. "Really?"

I turn my head towards the windshield again so that I don't have to face him. A little girl is chasing a purple ball into the street. Her hair is in braids with ribbons bouncing up and down as she runs and for some reason that makes me miss Lizzie even more.

"No, not really," I admit. "No, it's way more fucked up than that. I can't explain it to you. I wish I could. I just..." I shake my head. I just what? I don't even know. "Can things with us not be fucked up too?" I plead.

Spencer reaches over and puts a hand on my arm. "They aren't. I mean, they can be however we want them to be."

That sums up the real difference between the two of us. Spencer always seems like a sun that everyone else revolves around, able to bend the world to fit what he needs. I'm like some desolate planet that things keep crashing into without permission, leaving marks that can't be repaired.

"Yeah?" I ask. My muscles clench and for a minute, I'm afraid he's going to say no, that he's joking and that we're as fucked up as everything else seems to be.

But then he nods and says "yeah," and smiles, really smiles, and I'm amazed at how much better that makes me feel. He turns around and starts the car up and pulls us back onto Main.

"Just promise me one thing," he says with a serious expression.

I hesitate because given everything we've been talking about, I'm a little nervous about what he's going to come out with. But, I remind myself, it's not Lizzie, it's Spencer. He'd never do anything to hurt me. "Sure, what?"

"When you finally manage to kiss Ally, don't tell her if you enjoyed kissing me more. I don't think she'd take it that well."

For a second it feels like my blood freezes and Lizzie's heart stops. But then I watch Spencer dissolve in laughter. His laugh is so infectious I can't help but join him. I don't even remember the last time I've really laughed, and it feels so good that I almost convince myself that it's possible for him to be right. That maybe, at least between us, everything is okay.

Things at the hospital go well too, so maybe it's really possible for me to move on. My test results are good enough that I'm only going to have to come back every other week for the next month. Then once a month for the rest of the year to have a line put into my neck and tiny pieces of Lizzie's heart removed to be examined to make sure my body isn't attacking it.

No surprise to me, it doesn't look like my body is fighting off Lizzie's heart. The immunosuppressants I'm on are working. I don't think Lizzie wants to go anywhere.

After my appointment, Spencer picks me up and we head over to the mall. As much as I want everything to be back to normal, I think we both get that it isn't and I don't know what to do about that, so I avoid looking at him as much as I can.

The lot is crowded with weekend shoppers and people are driving stupidly like they always do at shopping centers. We're out on the far edge of the lot and I've switched with Spencer so I'm in the driver's seat. He didn't turn the car off and I can feel it humming beneath me. It shouldn't be any different than being a passenger, but I look out at the sea of other cars and people milling around and I realize that too much pressure on the gas and I might run into one of them. Or one of them will run into us. I can picture our car, Spencer's car, his favorite thing in the world, flipping with the impact. I can actually hear the scream of the sirens burning my ears.

I know Dr. Collins wouldn't be so happy now. I've

learned to recognize the telltale signs that mean my blood pressure is dangerously high. Lizzie's heart is racing and my temples are sore like a rod is being pushed from one side of my head to the other.

I don't know how long I sit there clenching the wheel and going nowhere. I'm paralyzed, dizzily watching this movie in my head of us in some terrible collision, one that Spencer can't walk away from this time, over and over. Just like the last one, this accident is my fault too. I don't get the car out of the way in time. Or my foot slips on the gas pedal and rams us into an oncoming truck.

There are too many things that can happen once I start moving the car. How could I not have seen that before? I have no control over this metal box at all and no one else does either. It's just random chance any of us drive a car and survive.

Spencer clears his throat and I realize I'd forgotten he was sitting next to me. He puts a hand on my arm and when he touches me, I jump so hard the only thing that keeps me in place is the seat belt.

"It's okay. We can do this another day," he says, trying to be comforting. But it doesn't matter if it's tomorrow or next week or even a month from now; nothing is going to be different next time I get behind the wheel.

I get out of the car on shaking legs and we switch seats. I shiver a little and strap myself in. For the first time I can ever remember, we don't talk all the way back to my house.

In fact, I don't even realize when we get there. Just suddenly, I'm aware that we aren't moving anymore.

"Thanks anyhow," I say to Spencer as I get out of the car.

The house looks like the only safe place for me. Solid. Unmoving. I bolt up to the door and stumble on the top step. Somehow Spencer is next to me, grabbing my arm to stop me from falling headfirst into the rose bushes Mom had put in last week. He trails behind me as I head to my room and stands there as I collapse down onto the bed.

"Do you still have that psychologist's card?" he asks.

I nod, but don't remember telling him about that. When I look up, he confesses. "Your mom told me. She wanted to know if I thought you needed to talk to someone."

I laugh even though nothing is funny. I can't believe that everyone has been talking behind my back about the fact that I seem to be cracking up. Even so, I'm actually relieved that Spencer is here, so I guess I can't really complain.

The bed dips as he sits down next to me and pulls out his phone.

"I'll make the appointment for you," he says. "I'll even go with you if it will help. I'll do whatever you want except sit here and watch you try to deal with all of this on your own."

"I'm not on my own," I protest. Even with all the weird shit going on, one thing Spencer Yeats has never made me feel is that I'm dealing with things on my own.

I won't leave you alone, either.

I'm not sure whether to smile or cry. Lizzie has gotten nicer since the accident, softer somehow. I want to reach out and hug her and inhale the turpentine in her hair. Instead I just wrap my arms around myself and glance up at Spencer. He's sitting next to me with his phone in his hand and a steely expression on his face.

"Cal." Spencer's voice is firm, waiting. He isn't going to let this go and I'm not sure I really want him to. Not anymore. Hearing Lizzie's voice is one thing. But last night … it can't happen again. And I can't stand the way I feel like I'm on the edge of something, waiting for a strong wind to push me over. I can't stand the worried look on Spencer's face. I'm tired of hurting the people I love the most.

I lean over the side of the bed, pull out my mitt, and hand him the card.

FOURTEEN

I curl the edges of the business card in my hand, wishing I hadn't promised Spencer that I'd go through with meeting Dr. Reynolds. I feel kind of stupid just standing outside the door, checking and rechecking the address. I'm balancing the pluses and minuses of either going through with the appointment or leaving and having to figure out how to face Spencer.

I mean, if all it took to be okay was to talk about things, I would talk to Spencer. Or even my mom if I was *really* desperate. So I wonder what type of miracle worker this guy is meant to be. Maybe he'll try to hypnotize me or just tell me that I'm acting like a dumb little kid who can't get over things and move on. Maybe he'll even call my parents and tell them not to ever let me drive again. And maybe I'd deserve that. Maybe I'd even thank him for it at this point.

When I finally go in, Dr. Reynolds' office is exactly what I was afraid a therapist's office would be. The waiting room has a few tables with a bunch of boring three-month-old magazines on them. There are a couple of uncomfortable, slightly stained couches pushed up against the wall and a few bookcases filled with dusty old books you couldn't pay me to read. I expect a secretary, but there's no one else here. Maybe that's a shrink thing. I'm kind of relieved, though. My mom already gave him all of our insurance info over the phone. The fewer people who know I'm here, the better.

By the time he comes out to call me in for my appointment, I'm just this side of a panic attack. I mean, the thing that scares me the most is not being able to prepare myself in advance and here I am getting ready to open myself up to someone I've never met, agreeing to answer questions that would have made Lizzie's look like a game.

As I debate whether to bolt or not, a girl bursts out of the door behind him. She looks like she was the practice subject for someone learning body piercing. Her eyes dare me to get out of the way so she can leave.

I move and seriously consider following her out, but curiosity gets the best of me and I look at Dr. Reynolds instead.

He's younger than I expected. Probably my parents' age and dressed in jeans and a button-down shirt. He looks like someone I'd see at a ball game, not like someone about to torture me with invasive questions I don't know how to answer.

"Cal?" he asks. "Having second thoughts?"

Or third, or fourth?

Lizzie wouldn't have seen a shrink. She wouldn't even see the counselors at school. The only person she ever talked to, aside from me and Spencer, was Mr. Brooks.

That's because he's hot.

I'm not even going to try to figure out if Mr. Brooks is hot or not. Besides, I know that isn't the real reason Lizzie felt like she could talk to him.

Dr. Reynolds is still waiting and this is my chance to bail. Being here isn't required; I've asked for this appointment. But I'm surprised to find that he looks so reasonable and relaxed. And whether I want to or not, I suppose I need to talk to someone besides Mom and Dad, who are already worried enough, and Spencer, who thinks he isn't doing enough to help me himself, and really, things with him are complicated enough.

"No," I say in a delayed response to his question, but somehow the word comes out in three syllables.

"Then come on in," he says with a smile, standing half-way inside his office, waiting for me to follow. I remind myself again I can leave at any time if I want to. Mom will pay for this regardless; she'll get it if I say it isn't for me. At least I think she will.

I follow him into his office and look suspiciously at the two chairs placed next to a small table. On the table are some sort of plant, a box of Kleenex, and two bottles of water. I do a quick sweep of the room and see he has the same calendar I do, the one with the '68 Tigers team on it.

"Lolich or McLain?" I ask as I walk over. The 1968 Tigers not only won the World Series but saved Detroit, which was in the middle of a series of race riots that year, from totally self-destructing. My dad bought me a set of DVDs that tell the story of what was going on during that time and it has all the series games on it.

That year, the Tigers had two pitchers who couldn't be more different. Mickey Lolich was the MVP of the series and not only allowed just five runs in three complete games, all of which he won, but hit the only home run of his six-teen-year career to win game two.

This was in contrast to Denny McLain, who went 31-6 with a 1.96 ERA and was the last pitcher to win more than thirty games in a season. He was named to the American League All Star team, and won the Cy Young Award for best pitching as well as the American League's MVP award. After, he fell apart in a series of gambling and organized crime allegations, which landed him in jail and by the time he was twenty-nine, he was out of baseball.

He was one hell of a player, but tried to live the life of a rock star and it backfired.

There's no right or wrong answer to my question, but if this guy is a fan, I need to know something about where he stands. He's about to learn a whole lot about me and I feel like I need to even the score.

"Does it have to be either/or?" Dr. Reynolds asks as he shuffles himself into a seat.

I keep staring at the calendar like it's the key to the universe. I'm tired. I want to sit down too, but I'm a bundle of nervous energy, a mess.

"No," I say. "But everyone seems to have a position." I walk around the small office feeling trapped by his lack of a definitive answer.

Still, I take a deep breath and force myself into the leather chair and distract myself by wondering about the girl I saw leave the office earlier and what her issues are.

"I like McLain," Dr. Reynolds says. "What he did in his personal life had nothing to do with how he pitched that year."

Hmmm…I nod. That's pretty much my thinking too. My dad discounts all of McLain's pitching accomplishments just because he was a screw-up off the field, but that never made sense to me. It wasn't like he took steroids or did any- thing that really gave him an edge in the game. One thing didn't have anything to do with the other. It was kind of like Lizzie's art. Some people didn't take her seriously because they thought she was strange and mouthy and not a great student. But really, she was so talented, they just couldn't see it.

"Cal, I know you have a lot going on, but you requested an appointment. Why don't you tell me what's on your mind, and we'll go from there."

I'm not prepared for him to be so open-ended. I was expecting an interrogation, so I hadn't planned anyplace to start.

Oh, Cal hasn't planned it all out. That's a first.

I shake my head and try to ignore her. "You know, right?" I ask Dr. Reynolds. "About the accident and all that?"

"Yes," he says. "And I'm sure you know *this*, but I want to be clear that anything you tell me is just between us. It doesn't matter who is paying your bills or who gave you my name. What's said in here stays here."

I nod. I know that from all the shows on TV, but it kind of helps to hear it. Still, my mind is a jumble of words and voices: mine, Lizzie's, even Spencer's. It's starting to get difficult for me to isolate which one is really mine. And even though I've been dreading his questions, I wish Dr. Reynolds would shoot some my way instead of putting all the pressure on me to figure out what to say.

"Do you know about Lizzie?" I ask.

"I know she was your friend. I know that she and your other friend ... " He looks down at the stack of papers on his lap. "Spencer, were close as well. I know she donated her heart to you. Is that what you mean?"

"Yeah, kinda," I say. "I mean, Spencer and I used to...I mean, Lizzie...she had this really screwed-up family, and we would look out for her. Ever since we were kids and no one really got it...not our parents or anyone or..." Suddenly, I'm breathing fast, and I can't seem to sort out my thoughts. I can feel Lizzie's heart beating double-time. I don't know if she wants me to talk or stay quiet, but I need to put everything in order and I can't do that on my own. She has to understand that. She just has to.

"Cal?" Dr. Reynolds says, and I realize he's been calling my name for a while and that I've been zoning out.

"Sorry," I say, staring at the floor. The carpet has these tiny brown and pink flowers on it that remind me of Lizzie. I take a deep breath and hold it in until my lungs hurt. The burning sensation feels better than the pain of missing her.

"That's okay. Slow down. Just tell me what you're thinking." His sincere expression makes it easy to believe he really gives a damn. He reminds me a little of Spencer and I figure, what the hell. I mean, what's the worst that can happen at this point?

"Lizzie had it really rough at home," I say, trying hard to streamline it all. "Spencer and I used to try to help her when we could."

He nods and somehow takes notes without looking down at his paper. "How old were you when you started helping her?"

I think back to the first time we'd gone over to her house to try to help her. "Nine or ten, I think."

A grimace crosses his face as he writes, but then his expression clears again. "And this continued until?"

"The last time was right before the SATs. Right before the accident."

He nods again. "Were you romantically involved with her?" he asks, but I say "no" before he can even finish the sentence.

"Did you want to be?"

"Of course not," I say, staring at my leg, which is bouncing up and down like it belongs to someone else. "She was in love with Spencer."

"Was it mutual?"

"Yes, but…" I hate this question. It's like when you're at the plate and waiting for a pitch; at some point you have to commit to swinging or not. You can't swing just a little. You can't unswing once you've gone for it. Once your wrist bends, that's it. You either hit the ball or you miss it, but either way you've swung the bat.

Whatever relationship Spencer and Lizzie did or didn't have isn't what I came here to talk about. And there's nothing Dr. Reynolds could say to get me to talk about the other night with Spencer. What's worse is, I'm not sure how to talk about one without the other anyway. I can't kind-of swing, so I settle for just the facts.

"He's gay. But they slept together. Once."

Dr. Reynolds doesn't miss a beat. "Did that upset you? That they were together and you were left out?"

I groan. At some level I was hoping a shrink might understand. Hoping there was one person in the world I wouldn't need to explain how our friendships worked.

"No," I say, "you don't get it."

"I'm sure I don't. But I'd like you to explain it to me."

I try to figure out how to make him understand. "See, I love both of them. I knew it really wasn't going to happen. Not really. But I actually kind of wanted them to get together. In a way, I mean."

Me too.

Lizzie's comment makes me smile even as I wonder how true my words are. Spencer and Lizzie always fit together. I just didn't want to be left out. Not that I'd say *that* out loud. I don't need Reynolds thinking I'm a total head case right off the bat.

"Why did you want them to be together?" he asks.

"Why did I want them to be together?" I just repeat his question, wrestling with feelings I'm not sure I understand. "It was always what she wanted," I say. "And Spencer loved her. They were good together. Good for each other." Lizzie's crazy sense of humor and daring escapades always made me nervous, but they seemed to bring out something similar in Spencer that he enjoyed and thrived on, even if he wouldn't quickly admit it.

"But Spencer is gay," Dr. Reynolds repeats.

"Yeah, he is. I knew they weren't going to go off and get married or anything. Lizzie knew that too, but … she … " I can feel the sting of tears burning behind my eyes, but I don't know why. I try to remember they're just facts. It's like reciting baseball stats or science equations. Facts can't hurt you. They're just a list of the way things are.

But then I have to wonder if maybe somewhere inside me it's Lizzie who is crying out, trying to figure out why Spencer loved her yet couldn't really be with her. I got what Spencer said about nothing changing between them, but I'm not sure anymore if that's even possible.

Dr. Reynolds holds out one of the boxes of tissues, but I shake my head and take a deep breath. I can do this.

"Cal, this appointment was made on"—he looks at his sheet again—"on Saturday. What happened that day?"

I bite the inside of my cheek to keep from laughing. I know there's nothing funny about this. I may not know what I want to say, but I definitely know what I don't want to say. So I cycle through all of the issues that got me to this point. Driving and the paralyzing fear I feel when I get behind the wheel. How to deal with killing one of your best friends. Lizzie and the damned stubbornness of hers that won't let her leave me the hell alone. Spencer and…everything.

My muscles knot up at once like they do after the first real workout of the season. The funny thing is, I really don't want to leave. So even though I'm shaking, I'm also trying to hold tight on to the arms of the chair to stop myself.

Dr. Reynolds reaches out slowly and puts his hand lightly on my arm, freezing me in place.

"I promise you," he says softly, "it will be much easier once you've said it. And there is nothing you need to be afraid to tell me."

"You're going to think I'm crazy." I realize as the words

come out of my mouth that this is really what I'm afraid of, that he'll think I'm nuts. What scares me the most isn't that I kissed Spencer, although *that's* never going to happen again. What scares me is that it was really Lizzie who kissed him. Lizzie who died. Lizzie whose heart and who knows what else is still inside me.

Reynolds smiles a small smile and holds up the stack of papers in his lap that obviously make up my file. "Cal, I know enough about you to know you aren't crazy."

He's dripping with sincerity, and I can see he believes what he's saying, but still I go back to the initial reason I came in to see him. "I can't drive. I get in the car and I can turn it on, but then I just sit there. I can't move. I'm scared. I killed her once and I don't want to do it again." My arms wrap around myself, my nails digging into my arms.

He doesn't hesitate before he responds. "You didn't kill her, Cal. I have the report right here. It wouldn't have mattered who was driving. The car that hit you was going eighty miles an hour when it hit that barrier. There was absolutely nothing you could have done."

I hear his words, but just like Spencer's, I can't process them. "She wasn't wearing her seat belt." I stumble over my own guilty words.

"And was there anything you could have done about that?"

"Sometimes I'd threaten not to leave until she put it on. Sometimes she'd listen and sometimes she wouldn't," I admit.

"Do you think she knew she should have been wearing it?" he asks.

"Of course, but Lizzie ... Lizzie was stubborn. She's still stubborn, she's ... " I stop, realizing I've broken my swing and totally missed the ball.

I draw my legs up onto the chair and wrap my arms around them. He might not think I'm crazy for not being able to get behind the wheel, but there's no way I'm comfortable telling him I can feel her inside me—like the heart that is keeping me alive is still hers and she's just loaning it to me.

"My file says you're a pretty exceptional ball player." He changes the subject so drastically it takes me a second to realize he's done it. It isn't a question, so I just nod.

"Shortstop?"

I nod again.

"Will you be able to play in the future?"

His question is so blunt that it takes me back. "I don't know. Not for the first year, anyhow. I'm on steroids. That would break league rules," I whisper. "After that, I don't really know." I'm waffling, but it's so freaking hard to have to say the words.

"That must be hard for you. But you know what else my file says?"

I shake my head and try to untangle my cramping legs.

"Science, Cal. I hear you're a very promising student."

You always follow the rules. You're such a good boy.

Lizzie's voice is mocking. She never understood my love of science and all things provable.

"You're lucky, you know; to be good at so many things," he says.

I think about it and maybe he's right. At least there's

something I love, not as much as baseball, but something else I'm good at.

"Cal, I know this is a difficult question, but what did you mean when you said you didn't want to kill Lizzie again?"

I look up at him and even though the tears aren't threatening anymore, my eyes are still stinging.

"I have her heart," I whisper, so softly I'm surprised he can hear me.

"I know," he says. "That's an incredible gift. She must have been a very special young woman to be thinking of those things at seventeen."

His words make me smile a little in spite of myself. I got so used to people putting Lizzie down for what they saw as her bad attitude or for her bohemian style. Only her art ever made people stop and think twice. But he's right. She was special. She still is. And I say so.

"Cal, you didn't kill her," he says, looking right into my eyes. His resolve reminds me of Spencer and his stare is so intense that it makes my whole body feel like it's on fire. I can't look away even though I want to. "I'd like you to come back in and talk to me again," he says. "Would you be willing to do that?"

I glance at the new watch my parents bought me to replace the one that was destroyed in the accident, and I can't believe the hour is over already. There's so much I want to let go of and we've only scratched the surface. I nod. He asks if Thursday is okay and then scribbles the time in his book.

"You have a ride home, right?" he asks.

"Spencer." Saying his name is almost more than I have energy for.

"Good," he says and smiles. "I'd like to meet him sometime, if that's okay with you."

"Maybe," I say.

"Yes. Maybe. But you I'll see on Thursday. Same time."

———————

Spencer is in his car waiting for me when I stumble out the door. I say "hi" but then just close my eyes and listen to him talk about the play and how Mr. Brooks is threatening to replace Laura as the lead. He mentions how much fun Ally has been at rehearsal and then pauses like he's waiting to see if I'm going to reply, but there's nothing I can say. I still don't know what's up with her and Dillard, and I'm not prepared to hear the answer if it's bad.

Spencer knows me well enough not to ask me anything about my appointment, or about how I'm feeling, or any of the other questions anyone else might have. He talks about school and shares some silly story about his brother going to a frat party. The sound of his voice calms me enough that by the time we're at my house, I can almost pretend that things are back to normal.

FIFTEEN

I used to manage fine juggling baseball practice, school, Spencer and Lizzie, and the occasional science fair. But now I almost need a secretary to keep it straight. Remembering to take all the pills I need, the appointments with Dr. Collins, the exercises I'm supposed to be doing, and now meetings with Dr. Reynolds, feels like a lot on top of school. It doesn't help that none of it truly feels like mine. It's all stuff I'm doing because people tell me that I have to.

I've added all the appointments onto my calendar, each in a different color, but I haven't erased the team's practice schedule. I keep going back and forth as to whether I should or not. Erasing it seems really permanent and I'm not ready to give up yet. But having those dates on the calendar, imagining the team out running drills, is torture.

During one of my late-night Internet searches I read about a guy who plays professional soccer even though he's had a transplant. I printed it off to show Dr. Collins, but he says there's no doctor in the world who would condone it. He made it very clear *he* never would.

And I've read about a golfer who has had three transplants and still plays professionally, but golf isn't the same as baseball. For most people, golf isn't a contact sport. I probably just need to give up, but I can't imagine never playing ball again. I don't want to imagine it. The best I can hope for is that I end up at a college with a good science program, a decent intramural league, and a coach who's willing to let me take the risk.

So when Coach Byrne corners me at school on Wednesday, it makes me a little uncomfortable. I'm on my way to lunch so I'm not in a hurry. I'm used to eating healthy during training, but the kind of diet I'm on now doesn't really inspire me to get to the lunch room faster than necessary.

"Don't look so excited, Ryan. You'll give the cooks a complex."

I worm my way through the rushing kids and over to a wall out of the flow. I'm pretty sure Coach isn't rushing to eat in the lunchroom either. "It's hard to build up a lot of excitement for lettuce."

He laughs. "Yeah, I'm sure. Actually, I'm hoping you can put off lunch for a few minutes. There's something I want to talk to you about." I wonder what use Coach could possibly have for me now. But I follow him out of habit, around the corner and into his office.

The room looks like probably every other high school coach's office. Trophies line the walls. Dusty framed pictures of past teams are hung in every other available space. Equipment litters the floor. On his desk are some baseballs and one of those Magic 8 balls that usually answers "ask again later" or "reply hazy, try again" when you ask it a question.

Over the years, I've spent a lot of time in here. Kids play school sports for a whole slew of reasons. At first, I played because I had a ton of time on my hands before my parents got home from work and I didn't want to stay at the after-school programs. Then I found out that not only was I good at baseball, but I actually loved it. And it wasn't just about playing. It was about the strategy and the numbers. I loved baseball like I loved science. It was safe, and structured, and it made sense.

I spent more hours than I could track talking to Coach about the best way to use our players while still meeting all the stupid league regulations demanding that everyone get a certain amount of playing time. But I have no idea what he wants to talk to me about now.

He gestures for me to take a seat.

"How're you feeling, kiddo?" he asks while he shuffles a bunch of papers on his desk.

"Fine, I guess." I push back in my seat, feeling both comfortable in this chair where I've spent so many hours and like I have no right to be here.

"We miss you, you know."

I squirm in the chair, not really knowing how to respond. I've never missed anything, aside from Lizzie, as much as I miss playing on the team.

Coach puts his papers down and links his hands together, leaning across his desk. "You've been a leader for this team for a long time, Cal. And not just on the field. You're one of the smartest players I've ever coached. Your head has always been in the game, and I think the guys are missing that influence."

Aw. They miss you, Cal.

My cheeks heat up with his praise and Lizzie's words. Coach Byrne isn't one for coddling his players, so I know he means it. The fact that they got clobbered on opening day probably doesn't hurt.

"Thanks." I look down at my hands, surprised to see they're tossing the baseball from Coach's desk back and forth. I wonder if I'll ever have a legitimate reason to hold a baseball again.

"Look. I don't want to eat up a lot of your time, so I'll get to the point. I've talked to the guys, and we'd like to know if you'd be interested in associating with the team in some way."

My hands stop moving and I grip the ball. Tight. "What?"

"Yeah," he says. "You know, set the lineups, talk strategy. If it makes any difference to you, it was pretty much a unanimous vote when I asked them how they felt about this."

"You mean, like be a student manager?" As I ask it, I realize it's perfect.

Coach nods. "Student manager. I like the sound of that. So, what do you say?"

There's really only one answer I can give. "Wow."

Coach smiles. "I figured you can run laps with the team when the doctors give you the okay. Lob a few around, work with some of the kids on their form, and we'd still get to use that brain of yours to sort out the hard bits. And I get that you'd have to plan around doctors' appointments and such. You know where we are when you can make it."

"Absolutely. Yes, thank you."

"No, thank you, Cal. Seriously, some of these kids need to get their heads out of... well, you know. Anyhow, let's aim for practice on Saturday. Usual time, if that works for you."

"See you then." I want to dance out the door. I know it isn't the same as actually playing ball but it's a hell of a lot better than sitting at home imagining I'm at practice.

———————

I bring the idea up to my parents at the end of dinner; dinner that involves food that's been cooked and not just reheated and with Mom, Dad, and me all sitting around the same table at the same time. That alone would make me happy if I wasn't already brimming over with excitement. But my joy is short-lived in light of the expression on my mom's face. My parents obviously aren't quite as convinced that this is a good idea.

"I don't know, Cal," Mom says. "I don't want you pushing yourself too hard."

Old Mom wouldn't have noticed if I'd trained for the Olympics. But this is new Mom. And new Mom, in comparison, is here all the time and making me crazy. I mean, I love her and all, but I'm used to a certain amount of autonomy, which seems to have been thrown out along with my old heart.

"Mom, it's a manager's spot. I'm not going to be turning double plays." I try to be matter-of-fact about it, figuring if I don't make it a big deal than maybe she won't either. I silently plead with Dad to jump into the conversation. We really haven't talked much since the night I found out about Lizzie's heart, but even so, he has to know what this means to me.

Dad looks from me to Mom. "Sheila, let's give him

a chance." He says it in such a way that I know it's his version of an apology. I hold my breath waiting for Mom's response. In our house, Dad might have an opinion, but Mom is the one to make the final call.

She sighs and gives me a "don't screw with me" look. "Cal, we'll try this, but you do not miss doctor's appointments and you don't get yourself overtired. And the minute Dr. Collins says it's too much for you, that's it. You're done. Do you hear me?"

I rush out of my chair and kiss her on the cheek and then give Dad a hug that takes him completely by surprise.

"Thanks. Thank you. Really," I say, smiling, which makes Mom smile.

Way to go, champ.

Even Lizzie's voice doesn't do anything to take away the joy of this moment. I rush upstairs and call Spencer. I know he's at rehearsal, but I'm so excited I'd rather leave a voicemail than wait until later. Then I pull out my glove from under the bed, put it in front of me on the desk, and start to plow through my homework, feeling lighter than I have in weeks.

SIXTEEN

I would have expected that my excitement at being part of the team again would make me dream about baseball. Or at least that Lizzie would let me enjoy tonight. But it's like she's feeling left out or something, because the dream I have is definitely not something my brain is generating on its own. And it's definitely not about baseball.

I remember reading once that nightmares are the brain's way of working out things you're too afraid to face when you're awake. That pretty much explains why I've never really had them. I'm intimately acquainted with all my fears; they don't really give me a break during the day so I think they sleep at night too. Anyhow, most of my dreams used to be about baseball and school, and stupid stuff like chasing a missing dog down the street. Oh, and if I got lucky, Ally.

But that was before. Now my dreams are filled with other things: dark tunnels and masked psychopaths driving tanks towards me; Lizzie's mom and her horrible assembly line of abusive asshole boyfriends. These dreams make me wake up covered in sweat and cowering in a twisted pile of covers.

And then there are the dreams about Spencer. Of course, Lizzie still likes to dream about Spencer.

I don't know what her dreams were like before they slept together, but these aren't as graphic as I would have guessed. I mean, she isn't *always* dreaming about having sex with him. Instead these dreams are worse than the terrifying ones because they're filled with so much sadness, I've actually woken myself up crying, bringing my mom charging into my room, probably worried I was dying.

Of course I can't fess up and tell Mom that I'm having Lizzie's dreams, and obviously talking to Spencer about them isn't an option. I suppose I could tell Reynolds, but given that he's the person most likely to have me committed, that's probably a stupid idea, so it's just me stuck with Lizzie's fantasies and grief.

Not only does it make seeing Spencer even more awkward in ways I can't explain to him, but I'm exhausted all the time because I'm spending too much time fighting against falling asleep. It's making it hard to concentrate in class too. I don't even realize it's Thursday until Spencer offers to drop me off at Dr. Reynolds' office after school.

The office is the same as it was when I left on Tuesday, only this time I know what to expect so I don't feel quite as stressed out. This time when he ushers me in, I sit down and start to make a list of the things in my head I *do* want to talk about.

There's the driving thing, of course. I mean, I can't ask Spencer to drive me around for the rest of my life, although knowing him, he'd do it. It's been fine since he hasn't brought up that night in The Cave again and neither have I. I just wish I could stop thinking about it. And doing an Internet search for "what do you do when you've made out with your best friend" is not going to get me anywhere. I can only imagine what Mom would think if she saw that in my browser history.

Then there's Lizzie. I've spent some time while I'm in school and Lizzie is … wherever she goes when she isn't actively in my head … thinking about it all. And I've made the decision that I have to find a way to talk to Reynolds about her before I go completely bonkers. I'm going to leave the dreams out of it. But at least I can talk about missing her. And maybe, if he seems cool, about the feeling that she's somehow still here with me.

"I'm glad to see you, Cal. I wasn't completely sure you'd want to come back," Dr. Reynolds says when he sees me. He's laughing a little and he really does look glad to see me.

"There are things I guess I really want to talk about," I admit.

"Go ahead then. What's on your mind?"

"It's Lizzie, really." I'm surprised at how guilty those words make me feel. It's like I'm reporting her to the principal or the cops.

"Yes?"

I have this speech in my head, but somehow the words keep tying themselves in knots between my brain and my mouth.

"I Googled it. I mean, what happens to people who are transplant recipients. People who get organs that belonged to someone else and who remember stuff … "

"Remember?" Dr. Reynolds cocks his heads and puts his stack of papers down. "Cal, are you talking about the theory of cellular memories?"

I nod. This is where he tells me I'm nuts; that Lizzie is dead and having her heart doesn't mean it's possible for some part of her to still really be alive inside me. My stomach flops and for a minute I worry that coming back here was a mistake. My shoulders tense as I glance at the door, calculating the best way to make a run for it.

"Interesting," he says. "So you feel like you're able to access Lizzie's memories?" He doesn't say this in the way I expected him to. It isn't that condescending response that means he's going to have me locked up. He actually sounds intrigued.

"No, not memories."

Yeah, be glad about that, Cal. You'd never sleep again.

"Dreams," I say, ignoring both her comment and my promise to myself to keep this a secret. "I've had dreams that I think are hers. And I can feel her. Inside me." I stop and blush because it sounds like I'm saying something suggestive when that isn't my intention at all. "Sorry. I'm not saying this right."

"It's okay, Cal. We're going to take this slowly. So you say you can feel her ... what, thoughts? Emotions? Even when you're awake?"

"Sometimes, I can feel her react to things." I'm kind of embarrassed to talk about it now. I've read report after report about people suddenly liking chicken when they'd been a vegetarian or bursting into tears when they listen to Frank Sinatra when they'd only listened to heavy metal. But I haven't really read anything about hearing voices or being influenced like what happened with Spencer.

"How does she react?" Dr. Reynolds asks.

"It's like I can feel her heart race in reaction to things.

I can kind of sense when she's happy or upset. And I hear her voice almost like she's talking to me, only I know that I can't really be hearing it. And sometimes, it's like she wants to do something and . . . "

"Her heart?" he asks with a raised eyebrow. "Do you feel like she's made you do things you don't want to do?"

"No . . . I . . . It isn't like that. She just . . . I don't really want to talk about it. I thought I did, but . . . " I say, too quickly. I'm pissed at myself because I've just said everything I wasn't going to. I thought I could talk to him about Lizzie without talking about Spencer and everything else, but it's all tied up together and it isn't working.

And really, at the end of the day, all I want is to be able to get in the car and drive like a normal person. I want to not be afraid that I'm going to kill someone every time I'm behind the wheel.

"Okay, that's fine. We'll talk about what you're comfortable with. Do you want these feelings to go away?"

I try to figure out how to untangle the mess of thoughts in my head. "It doesn't really bother me all the time. I mean, it's like she isn't really totally gone and that's nice. It's nice to have her with me. I miss her. I just . . . "

I miss you too, you know.

"Do you feel like sometimes it's too much?"

"Yeah. Something like that." I look around for something to do with my hands. I wonder if this is how Spencer feels when he's onstage and how he could possibly like it. I hate that feeling of being watched except when I'm on the field. I get up and walk over to his desk and pick up a ball encased in plastic, black signatures flowing over it.

"That's the 1984 team," he says. It's pretty cool that he has all of this historic baseball stuff.

"My coach … my old coach … asked me to be student manager of the varsity team," I say. I hope it will balance all of the stuff about me that's probably in that paperwork and all the bizarre stuff I've told him today. Maybe it will make him realize that I haven't turned into a total loser.

"That sounds like it would be good for you. Are you going to do it?"

"Sure." I try to downplay the excitement I'm feeling to be doing something that involves baseball, but then it wells up and spills over through the smile that widens my mouth. "I start on Saturday."

I put the ball down and go back to the chair and sit, more relaxed now. "See, it's just that Lizzie is braver than I am. Lizzie … nothing really scares her. It never really did. And I feel like I owe her."

Dr. Reynolds nods and plays with his pen. "Cal, before the accident, did you ever feel like Lizzie pushed you into doing things?"

"I guess that depends on what you mean by pushed," I say. "I mean, she was always trying to get me and Spencer to do crazy things with her. She just liked to have fun. And I think … no, I know, she enjoyed making me squirm, which is pretty easy to do."

"And now?"

"Well, no I wouldn't say she's pushing me. Most of the time it's just these surges of feelings, except for … " Crap, I've done it again and I'm not talking about that. I don't care how cool this guy is and how much great baseball stuff he has. I'm not talking about Spencer.

"Except for?" Of course, he doesn't miss anything.

"Nothing," I say, wondering when the hour will be over.

"These surges of feeling. Are they frightening?"

"No…I mean, it's just Lizzie. But it's distracting sometimes and we don't always feel the same way about things."

Ain't that the truth!

Reynolds leans forward. "Cal, you're dancing around something here that I think you want to talk about but are afraid to. You know you can tell me anything, right? I'm not judging you. I'm here to help you work through all of this."

"Can we talk about driving?" I know that it isn't an answer to what he's said, but I feel like if I keep talking about Lizzie, I'm going to crack in two and not even the doctors will be able to put me back together.

"Of course. We can talk about whatever you want."

"It isn't getting easier. I mean, every time I even think about getting in the car I'm worried that I'm going to kill someone."

"You know that isn't likely, right?"

"The odds are one in 19,000." I know this because I looked it up. I tried to find the odds of getting a heart transplant at sixteen, but it must be so rare that they haven't been calculated.

"What do you think would have happened had Lizzie or Spencer been driving the car that day?"

His question stumps me. It was one I hadn't thought to ask. "I don't know. Lizzie drove like a maniac, and Spencer…I don't know."

"I have a copy of the accident report here," he says, pulling out a dog-eared sheet of paper from the middle of his pile. "Has anyone shown it to you?"

I shake my head.

"Would you like to see it?" He holds it out to me. I hesitate for a minute. I've done everything possible to avoid hearing the details or knowing anything about the guy in the other car. But I'm curious about what he thinks might help me, so I take it.

There are a lot of things written down, like mile-markers and license plate numbers. To my relief, the other driver's name has been crossed through with black magic marker, but in the "notes" box it says "distracted driver: cell phone text."

Okay, the guy that hit us wasn't paying attention. I get it.

Dr. Reynolds is looking at me expectantly, waiting for something to sink in. "I don't want to preach to you, but did you know that over nine people a day are killed in the US alone by distracted drivers?"

I shake my head.

He looks down at his papers and muses, "It's the leading cause of death for teens."

"Was the driver a kid?" The question doesn't feel like my own. I really don't want an answer. None of that matters. But I can feel Lizzie's curiosity rising. She'd want every last detail. "Never mind. I don't want to know."

Dr. Reynolds pauses and looks at me. "It might help you come to terms with things," he says. "If you did want to know. When you're ready."

I shake my head as he reaches over and takes the

paperwork back before I have a chance to read the rest of it. I'm sure somewhere on there are a bunch of other things I don't want to know: details of how they had to pry me out of the car and where they found Lizzie.

"And we *can* review that, Cal. But until then, try to accept that it wasn't your fault," he says again, as if repeating it enough times will push it through the wall in my brain that's keeping me from being able to accept it.

I nod. I almost believe it when he says it so emphatically. He looks down at his book and cocks his head. "Tuesday? Do you want to come back Tuesday?"

I think about it and am almost surprised that yes, I do want to come back. It's easy to talk to him. I might not be jumping in the car when I get home, but I can breathe a little easier than I could when I came in.

"Okay."

"Can I ask you to do one more thing?" he asks. "I'd like you to keep a journal."

"Like a diary? I'm not really a writer."

"That's okay. I'm not suggesting that you write a book. But I'd like you to make a list of every time you think Lizzie is … with you. Influencing you. Every time you think you can feel her thoughts."

My stomach goes sour. Putting things in writing scares me. There's something permanent, something public about that. Something I'm not sure Lizzie wants. Something I'm not sure I want.

"Dr. Reynolds … " I start to beg off.

"You don't have to, Cal. You don't have to do anything.

But I'm going to suggest it might help you to get a handle on which areas of your life you feel she's having the most control."

I hear what he's saying, I really do. I just don't know that I actually want to do it. "Can I think about it?"

"Of course," he says, already working on something else. "See you on Tuesday."

SEVENTEEN

Reynolds' list is a lot harder than it sounds.

I keep taking out pieces of yellow lined paper like the ones I used to use to write down my baseball career options, and stare at them, willing the words to appear.

I try to catalog the times when I think Lizzie's heart is pounding because she's reacting to something. And I write down the crazy dreams that are definitely not mine. I even force myself to describe the flicker of feelings that go through me when Spencer and I are just hanging out.

But I feel stupid. Even though no one has seen the list, it makes me feel self-conscious. There are a whole lot of balled-up pieces of yellow paper in the garbage can next to my desk from lists I've started and destroyed. And there are a bunch of ashes in the can from the earlier pieces of yellow paper that I've already burned. The last thing I need is my mom reading what I've written. Or Spencer finding them.

It's much easier to blow off the lists and focus on Saturday and the weather. The forecast is 65 degrees and sunny with light winds blowing from behind the plate. That's perfect weather for baseball in a part of the country that could just as easily see snow in April.

The team will practice inside if the weather turns bad, but I don't want to sit inside the stuffy gym. I want to be on the field, smelling the freshly cut grass and feeling the sun on my skin. I don't want to watch everyone run laps inside. I want to hear the sound the ball makes when it hits the glove. I want to hear the crack of the bat.

I'm too keyed up to sleep much on Friday night. I stay quiet, though, because I don't want Mom to know I'm awake or she'll decide that I'm getting too excited and make me come home after my appointment at the hospital. She doesn't get that it's a good thing; that even though I won't be playing, the thought of standing on a baseball diamond energizes me.

I get to the field early on Saturday because Mom drops me off after my checkup. The doctor is still happy and says I can kick up my exercises, which is great because the meds are making me bloated and even the thought of running makes me feel light and free.

I'm so early there are only two cars in the lot. One I know is Coach Byrne's, but I don't recognize the other one, which is a small blue convertible. I wander over to the field and find Coach sitting in the bleachers. He's sorting through line-up cards filled with player stats and projections against the standout pitchers in our league.

I'm way happier than I should be to see these lists of names and numbers. It's probably strange to love trying to make the numbers come out in our favor almost as much as I love playing. I pick up the first card in his stack and convince him to move a couple of the guys around in the batting order. I know the pitcher we'll probably be facing for our first game and he has a crazy screwball that some of our usual guys are going to try to slam. They're going to fail miserably.

While he's filling in his sheets, I watch the grass move

in the breeze. It feels like summer and home and while I want to be out there playing, I'm grateful to be here at all.

"This is the best decision I've ever made," I say to Coach without tearing my eyes from the field.

"Good thing you're young. You have time to make even better ones," says a girl behind me.

I turn around and realize that after all of this time, I'm somehow having a conversation with Ally Martin.

She's wearing slightly faded jeans with a long-sleeved white T-shirt and a Central Warriors baseball cap over her long hair, which she's pulled back. I have a freaky flashback to one of the Ally/baseball dreams I haven't had in so long and then stand there without a coherent thought running through my head. I literally have nothing. For her part, she's smiling, but there's a challenge in her eyes. I think she knows how much this is bugging me out.

Finally Coach looks up and says, "Oh, not sure if you two know each other. Cal Ryan. Ally Martin. Ally is our official scorekeeper this season. I wanted her to get a little practice in too." Coach is calm, like he can't tell that worlds have just collided in front of me.

"Scorekeeper?" I ask, like I've never heard the concept before.

Ally sits down next to me and puts her feet up on the row of the bleachers in front of us. "Yup. Coach needed someone and I've got experience, so here I am."

My brain is being pulled in two because I couldn't ask for anything better—if more distracting—than to have baseball and Ally at the same time. But I can't imagine what experience she could have. The official scorekeeper spot always has a million people applying for it since they actually have a certain amount of power in a game. They determine what's an error and what's a hit. They keep all the stats. I have no idea how Coach is possibly going to teach her everything before the season opens. I realize it's my turn to speak, but I'm not sure if I should be worrying about talking to her because I've wanted to for so long or worrying about her being our scorekeeper.

"Stop looking so terrified, Cal," she laughs. "You know my dad coaches the Central College Warriors, right? I've been doing this for their team the last few years."

Her dad coaches the best private college baseball team in the state. How the hell did I not know that? I know a million useless things about her. I know what her favorite flavor of yogurt is. I know what bands she likes, and what books she reads. I don't know how I managed to miss this.

I replay the sound of her saying my name. I'm having one of those moments that I want to capture so I inhale and try to hold it in, the bright sun, this freshly mowed grass, and the faint smell of vanilla.

I don't really know what my face looks like when I do this, but Ally, who amazingly is sitting next to me and speaking to me, puts her hand on my shoulder, where it feels like it burns a delicious hole through my shirt.

"Are you okay?" she asks.

"I'm fine," I say. "Never been better." And it isn't really a lie.

She has an easy laugh and it kind of explodes out of her. "Oh, good. So who's filling in for you at short?"

My stomach twists. "Dillard, I guess." Coach nods distractedly in agreement. Suddenly I wonder if there's any way I could talk Coach into letting me play. I want Ally to see what I can do on the field. I want her to see me as more than just heart transplant boy who has to sit on the sidelines.

And then I remember the conversation I overhead in the hallway. She's probably doing this to spend more time with Dillard. But before I have time to torment myself with that thought, she utters the most amazing words I've ever heard.

"Justin has a nice swing, but he doesn't have your hands."

I look down at my hands, which are holding the line-up sheets and shaking from adrenaline and nerves. It's like I'm seeing them for the first time.

"You've seen me play?" I ask. And then wish I could take it back because I'm sounding like an insecure suck-up.

"Of course. I've come to most of the games."

It's the strangest thing to be having a conversation with her. All the fear that's been built up over the past year sits like a hard ball in my stomach, but somehow, I'm able to push through it. It baffles me how I could have possibly missed seeing her at our games. Probably for the best. I can't imagine that knowing she was there would have helped my batting average.

I want to ask her about whether she and Dillard are together, but the team starts to gather. Everyone comes up and pats me on the shoulder and says how glad they are to have me back and hopes I'm doing well and all of that. For a minute I don't mind being the center of attention.

I catch Dillard staring at Ally. He looks like he wants to eat her for lunch.

Finally, Coach stands up and tells everyone to shut up. "Okay, everybody, welcome to spring. This is where you get to redeem yourselves for that poor excuse for an opener last week. So let's see ten laps and then we're going to try some fielding drills." There's general mumbling and grumbling, but everyone picks themselves up and heads down to the field.

"Coach, is it okay if I join in?" I ask. I'd wanted to run with the team anyhow and now I've got so much energy racing through me that I feel like I need to burn it off just to function.

Coach gives me the once-over and then nods. "Go. But don't overdo it. And I mean that," he says, sounding way too much like my mom.

I start down the bleachers and hear, "Hey, wait up." When I turn around, Ally is following me.

Of course I stop and wait for her. She takes off her shoes. My jaw drops as she unbuttons her jeans and starts sliding them off, revealing a tight pair of black running shorts. I wonder how I'm possibly going to be able to get through this. I'm suddenly so turned on I'm not sure I can walk much less run. It's like the blood in my body isn't even sure where it needs to be. It's just scattered as far from my brain as it can get.

Lizzie's laughter circles around me—of course she'd be loving this—until I turn away from Ally and focus on taking long, slow breaths while I stretch out.

"Meet you out there," Ally calls over her shoulder.

I stop mid-stretch and watch her as she slips back into her shoes. I'm amazed at this day. Amazed at how lucky I feel in spite of everything.

The team flies by us, but I don't care. For the first couple of laps, Ally and I pace each other without saying anything. My muscles are sore and it feels like it's been forever since I actually did anything real with them. I know I'm going to hurt like hell tomorrow, but it's hard to care.

On the next go-round Dillard slows down and runs alongside us.

I focus on my feet hitting the grass. The last thing I want to do is get into some sort of pissing match with him in front of Ally.

She pulls ahead as he tries to throw an arm around her. But then she elbows him sharply in the ribs and says, "Get the hell off me."

"Aw, honey," he whines, "why do you have to be that way?"

I'm ready to take him down if he steps out of line, but she seems to be able to handle him. When he stumbles, I speed up and pass him, drawing level with Ally again.

"You don't want to get too close to Ryan," Dillard calls behind us. "You know he's queer for Yeats." He draws Spencer's name out like it has a hundred "s's" in it, like it's being said by a snake.

My hands ball into fists. If Ally weren't here I'd haul off and slug him again, even though it would probably get me thrown off the team for good, not to mention that a proper fight could kill me and if it didn't, Spencer probably would if he got wind of it.

Thankfully, Coach spots that Dillard has slowed down to hang with us and takes matters into his own hands. "Dillard, get your butt in gear or it'll be warming the bench this season."

Dillard has no choice but to race ahead. First, though, he winks at Ally, which just causes her to roll her eyes.

I'm sure she's heard all the rumors about Spencer, me, and Lizzie. Everyone has. I just have to hope she's smart enough not to believe them. Before she can say anything, I throw out the crucial question. "So are the two of you...?" I point to Dillard, but leave the sentence hanging because I don't even want to say it out loud. I just power ahead, not even looking at her. So when she stops dead in her tracks—literally stops—it takes me a minute to notice and I have to double-back for her.

She looks hurt and angry, like I've seriously offended her. "What? No. How could you even think that?"

I jog in place and motion for her to start running. "Sorry, I just thought..."

"That I had really horrible taste in boys? Because seriously, he's the biggest dick I've ever met."

I give her a sheepish grin. "Sorry. Really. I won't make that mistake again."

She smiles back as if she knows something I can't possibly understand. "No. No you won't."

Then she starts running again, and leaves me in the middle of the field wondering what the hell is going on

EIGHTEEN

1. ~~I have a dream where I'm Lizzie and she's dancing with Spencer. She really likes it and …~~
2. ~~When I was talking to Ally, I felt this push to kiss her. Only we were just talking. I'm not ready to kiss her yet, but Lizzie was always trying to get me to move faster.~~
3. ~~Spencer and I were in his car and …~~

Every list I write for Dr. Reynolds sounds stupider than the last, so I just keep crossing things out.

I flip the paper over. My writing is small and spidery and I don't really have the courage to title it. But it's a new list of things about Ally. I'm embarrassed to put anything down on paper, but in the same way that writing my Lizzie-list makes all of the strange things happening more real, making a list of things about Ally makes *that* more real too.

Some of the things I've written down are things I've just learned. Some are things that I've known all along from watching her over the past year and all of them make me happy.

1. Baseball!
2. She smells like vanilla.
3. Her dad coaches the Warriors.

4. She's read all the Harry Potter books.

5. She's seen some of my games. (Hopefully that includes the one where I hit the grand slam!)

6. She eats egg salad sandwiches for lunch twice a week.

7. She's joined the drama club to get her arts requirement.

8. Her mom died when she was a kid and she's an only child like me.

9. She's funny.

10. I think it might be easy to ~~fall in love~~ be friends with her.

I don't show either list to Dr. Reynolds. He doesn't ask to see my Lizzie list, which is fine because I don't have anything I want to show him. Besides, I've had fewer of Lizzie's bad dreams this week and thankfully none about Spencer. I'm not ready to share my facts about Ally either, so maybe I'm good.

Instead he teaches me some deep breathing techniques. Things I can do to calm myself down when I get too worked up, like counting to a hundred, calculating baseball stats, or reciting the periodic table in order, which is something I've been doing since I was a kid. I just didn't realize why.

We talk about my appointments with Dr. Collins and how well they're going. We talk about practice. We talk about driving and he tells me again and again that the accident wasn't my fault. We don't talk all that much about Lizzie and we pretty much never talk about Spencer.

Before I know it, it's Saturday again and I'm back on the baseball field.

"So, as some of you know," Coach Byrne says at the end of practice, "I've got a long-running feud with the coach of Fairview." I know what's coming but most of the team looks confused. He pauses before delivering the punch line. "He's my brother." Everyone laughs, but they wouldn't if they knew that while Coach Byrne might be a nice guy, that goes out the window where his brother is concerned. The two of them are seriously competitive about everything: where they live, the grades their kids get, and mostly, the success of their baseball teams. Plus, the Fairview High Demons are the team to beat in our league. And with our current lineup, we don't even come close and Coach knows that.

"Anyhow, so next Saturday instead of coming here and taking it easy, I want you all to get your sorry butts over to their field and try not to let them wipe the floor with you. The game doesn't count in the standings but I guarantee you that if you make me look bad in front of my baby brother you are not going to be happy campers. Got it?"

Everyone nods in unison.

I feel a serious pang go through me. It isn't a physical pain, but it's an ache not unlike what Lizzie saddles me with when I'm around Spencer. I want to play in this game so badly it hurts. But I know no matter how much I beg Dr. Collins, it isn't going to happen. Even if he agreed, which he won't, I'd have to get through my mom and that door is shut tight.

The team goes off to the showers or home or wherever,

and I'm left sitting here looking out over the field that I can no longer play on.

I'm glad to be on the field at all, but I can't help thinking about how Dillard is no match for Fairview. He's too arrogant to wait out their starting pitcher and he's a mess in the field and the Demons know that. Plus they're going to hit up the middle with their wicked bats and he's going to let every one of those line drives through. No amount of strategizing on my part is going to save them. There's no one else on the team who can play short.

"You look lost in thought." Ally sits down next to me. I'm getting used to seeing her like this, in a T-shirt and shorts, but the effect of it hasn't diminished. She still takes my breath away, and not just physically. Knowing we have this bond over something that matters so much to me just ramps everything up.

I shrug. There's no point in my whining about not being able to play. Not when Lizzie can't paint, or kiss, or laugh. Not when Lizzie can't do anything.

Yeah, got it, Cal. You can stop using me as an excuse now. No sense both of us having no life.

"Do you think there's any chance we'll beat Fairview?" Ally asks, but I suspect she already knows the answer.

"Not a hope in hell," I answer honestly. Not only do they have the highest on-base percentage of any team in our league, they have a few pitchers who I swear were either held back so many times that they should already be in college or were recruited from other schools. That's just my theory. No one has been able to prove anything.

"I think I could field the ball against them better than Justin," she says. Even though I know they aren't together, at some really juvenile level it makes me happy to hear her putting Dillard down.

"Yeah, our only chance would be to put Velcro on his mitt and hope the ball finds its way into it."

She laughs and then her face gets all serious. "Do you think they'll ever let you play again?"

I get why everyone is asking me that, but I'm tired of having to think about what I can't have. Still, it's Ally, so I answer her question.

"Yes and no. Hopefully I'll be able to take it easy and play intramurals, but not varsity so I'm not sure it's worth it. And no contact, so forget about sliding or bashing into the catcher at home; what's the point?"

She doesn't say anything false to try to make me feel better. She just says, "That sucks," which actually does make me feel better because it's true and because it means she gets it.

I squint up at her. The sun is playing on the little hairs that stand up all around her head. I love that she isn't one of those girls who looks like she spends hours getting ready before she'll leave the house. I love that she seems so kind. I think about all of the things I like about her, until I hear *Gag* from Lizzie and "Hey, so can you pick me up on Saturday?" from Ally.

"What?" I know what Lizzie means, but I'm in shock to realize that Ally Martin is asking me to pick her up, which probably means taking her home too, not to mention spending the half an hour in the car each way to and from Fairview together.

Yeah, sport. But you still haven't gotten behind the wheel of a car and made it... you know... move.

Crap. Lizzie is right, but Ally doesn't know any of this, so she answers like I obviously didn't understand what "pick me up" means.

"My car is going into the shop on Wednesday. Can you give me a lift to the game? I'll buy you dinner after to pay you back for the gas, if you don't have any plans."

My face is on fire and my brain isn't processing things quickly enough. But even through my temporary insanity I realize that I'd get to spend all day with her. All I need to do is to drive the damned car, something I've done hundreds of times in the past and something that now absolutely terrifies me to the depths of my soul.

There's a loop in my brain that's pushing these thoughts around and around like a merry-go-round on crack. I feel like a little kid in a toy store; a huge ball of "want." Everything is just sitting there, waiting for me to reach out and take it, and all I can think of is the accident, and Lizzie, and my heart—Lizzie's heart—is starting to race.

Buck up, Cal. Time to be a big boy.

I know I'm meant to say, "Sure, what time is good?" or something else casual that doesn't make it sound like I've dreamt of having this conversation a million times before. But I can't open my mouth because my teeth are clenched so tightly that my jaw is aching. Inside, Lizzie's heart is beating like a clock ticking down the seconds before I blow this one chance.

"Oh," Ally says, looking disappointed at my silence.

"Will they not let you drive yet?" She's obviously throwing me a lifeline I don't deserve.

"No, that's not it." I instantly regret my honesty because that would have been the best excuse I could have hoped for. "I … I'm … " I look at her and what the hell can I say to this girl? That I'm so scared of doing to her what I did to Lizzie? That I'd be less afraid of holding a loaded gun to her head?

"It's okay," she says, staring out at the empty field. "I didn't mean to push. Sorry. I can find another way there."

She sounds disappointed and it's killing me that I'm pissing on the chance to spend some time with her. So instead of saying that I'll meet her there and asking either Mom or Spencer to drive me, and instead of telling her the whole truth because who knows what she would think of that, I take a big gulp of air and force myself to say, "No, it's good. Just tell me what time." It's a performance even Spencer would be proud of.

She breaks into a wide smile that lights up her face and leans over and kisses me on the cheek. Half of me wants to scream in joy and half of me wants to scream in terror. I'm honestly not sure which side would be louder.

NINETEEN

And that's how I find myself behind the wheel of Spencer's car on Tuesday, heading to see Dr. Reynolds. My parents said they'd replace my car with the insurance money *if* I'm actually going to drive. But I have to prove myself before they'll spend the money.

And Spencer is on a crusade. He's determined to find a way to get me over my fear. His current plan is to bribe me to drive to my appointment today. And my reward for doing that is getting to borrow his precious Sweeney on Saturday to go see Dr. Collins and then to pick up Ally for the game.

I'm committed to doing whatever it takes to make that happen. But it's easier said than done and as soon as I'm behind the wheel, the now-familiar terror washes over me. I go from calm to clammy and huffing for air in under two minutes.

Lord, Cal. Just drive the damned car already.

Lizzie is impatient, which is making me more anxious, and finally Spencer reaches over and turns off the car.

He thinks for a minute, then asks, "What do you have faith in?"

"What?" I haven't the foggiest idea of what he's talking about.

"Some people have faith in religion, or fate, or love, or whatever. What do you have faith in?"

I look at Spencer, who is probably what I have the most

faith in, but there's absolutely no chance of my saying that out loud.

"I don't know. Science, I guess. Cause and effect?" I offer because it seems as good as any.

Spencer nods and sits back in his seat. "Fine. So what's the science of driving a car?"

My head fills with visions of pistons, and valves, and intake systems, but I know that Spencer couldn't care less about how a car works. "You really don't want me to go into all that, do you?"

A grin spreads across his face. "No, not really. I just want you to think about it."

"Fine. I'm thinking about it," I say sarcastically, but from the look on his face I can tell that I'm still missing his point.

"Calvin," he exclaims in an exaggerated whiny voice that he learned for a show and that would make my skin crawl even if his use of my full name didn't.

I take my hands off the wheel. "I hate that, you know."

"Yeah, I know." He laughs. "Perhaps I'm just going to call you Calvin until you get this thing moving."

I think of transmissions and fuel injection processes and of having to hear Spencer calling me "Calvin" for the rest of my life, then I turn the key and try to think about nothing while I back us out of the driveway.

———

I drive like a five-year-old on his first bike. I wish the car had training wheels. By the time I get us to Dr. Reynolds' office, I'm a shaky mess and even Spencer is looking a bit green when I stop the car.

He wanders down the block to get food, or maybe tranquilizers for the trip home. I turn the other way and head up to see Dr. Reynolds. The newest yellow piece of notebook paper, the one I haven't thrown out yet, that I haven't decided whether to show him, is crammed into my back pocket.

I'm still a little shaky when I get to the office, which Reynolds of course notices.

"You look pale, Cal. Are you okay?"

"Yeah." I take my usual seat. "I just drove here and … it was hard."

"I bet. Did you come alone?"

"No, it's Spencer's car. He came with me."

"Well, that's good. That's a step in the right direction. It will get easier from here." Dr. Reynolds seems so certain, but then he doesn't know yet about my promise to Ally.

"That's what I want to talk to you about. Driving, I mean. I expected it to be easier with Spencer, once I could actually do it. I'm always relaxed around Spencer. Well, usually." And then I laugh a little because my hands are still shaking and there's no way that I look relaxed. "Well, more relaxed than with anyone else."

"And it *will* get easier, the more you do it." That makes sense, but … even before the accident spending time with Ally probably would have made me a bundle of nerves.

"Yeah, maybe. But what about having other people in the car?"

"Like who? Your mom?"

"No. There's this girl." And I tell him the whole story about Ally transferring to our school and how I haven't been able to take my eyes off her, but never had the nerve to talk to her until we were thrown together on the team.

"I'm curious what was keeping you from speaking to her before. You aren't normally shy around girls, are you?"

I think about it. "No, but Ally...I...I'm not sure I totally understand it myself. I just thought she was out of my league. And then there was Lizzie..."

"Lizzie? But I thought you weren't interested in her as a girlfriend."

"I'm not. I wasn't. Lizzie was always telling me to talk to Ally." I think back to the night at the theater when I was watching Ally and all of the vulgar suggestions that Lizzie was making to creep me out. "But, it's just...right before Ally moved here I went out with this girl once."

I have to sift through my memories to come up with her name. "Karen. Her mom and my mom worked together and for some reason they thought it would be a good idea for us to meet. She was okay. My mom dropped us off at a movie. And halfway through, my phone started vibrating. I tried to ignore it but it didn't stop, so I went out into the lobby to check it. It was Spencer. Lizzie had called him. She found her mom unconscious and couldn't wake her up. She'd called 911, but..."

"You felt like you had to go over there?"

"I did. Of course I did."

"Why?" he asks.

His question blanks out my brain. It's like the way that

old scoreboards used to be cleared, each board clacking back to a black space where a number used to be. There's nothing in his question for my mind to grasp onto. I don't even get it. "What do you mean, 'why'?"

"Well, why did you have to go over there? She'd done the right thing by calling 911 and Spencer was going over there, so why did you feel like you had to leave your date to be with her?"

"Because Lizzie was my friend," I sputter out. My chest is pounding like I've been running laps. I'm not sure what he's getting at, or what he thinks I was supposed to do, or how he could have expected me to sit in the movie theater with this girl I didn't even know when Lizzie needed me.

"So if one of the guys on your baseball team had called you, would you have left the theater?"

"No, probably not," I say, frustrated. "You aren't getting it." What little sense of accomplishment I was feeling from driving has evaporated. I launch up from the chair and walk over to the window. I let the leaves of the plant run through my fingers and concentrate on breathing until I think I can talk without wanting to punch something.

Dr. Reynolds hasn't moved. When I turn around I take another shot at explaining it to him.

"It was Lizzie. I couldn't just watch that stupid movie with this girl I didn't even know when Lizzie needed me. Don't you understand that?" I thought I'd calmed down a little but I'm surprised to feel that my cheeks are getting hot and my eyes are stinging again. I don't know what it is about this damned office that makes me feel like crying every time I'm here.

"Come sit down and try to relax, okay?"

I do as he says and then take a stab at stringing the words together. "Spencer and I had our families. We had each other. We had other friends. She didn't. She just had us. And we promised we'd always take care of her. I wasn't going to bail on that just to watch a movie."

"How did the girl you were with react?" he asks.

I think back, but I don't really remember because I guess I didn't really care. Staying wasn't an option.

"I think she was pissed. She had to call her mom to come get her. I never saw her again. I just told my mom that we didn't hit it off."

Wow. I never knew that. I'm sorry, Cal.

"So you were worried that the same thing would happen with this girl? Ally?"

His question makes me stop and think. Could Lizzie have been the reason why I was too afraid to talk to Ally?

"I didn't want it to. I really, really wanted to talk to her. I wanted to ask her out. I thought about it every time I saw her. Every day. But I just didn't know how to do it."

"Because you might have to leave her to be with Lizzie?"

Blame it on me. Seriously, it doesn't matter anymore.

"Maybe. And," I admit, as much to Lizzie as to Reynolds, "because I was scared of screwing it up."

"But now Lizzie isn't around and Ally seems interested in you."

It isn't a question, and I'm glad, because I hadn't thought about it like that. I mean, what would have happened had Ally started talking to me before the accident? It adds a whole other layer of guilt onto what I'm already feeling and it's the first time I've really regretting talking to Dr. Reynolds.

"Cal?"

"Yeah, sure, whatever," I say, trying to push all of his words out of my head. I can't have Ally wrapped up in the guilt that's already overwhelming me.

"So you're upset because a girl that you're interested in is interested in you?"

"No. I'm happy about that."

"So what is it that's really worrying you?"

Finally, we get to it. The whole point of my coming today. "Like I said, I told her I'd pick her up, but I can't imagine how I'm going to be able to do it. How I'm going to drive with her in the car without losing my shit."

"Did you think of telling her the truth? That you're scared of driving?" Dr. Reynolds asks me.

"Of course. I just don't want to be that guy. The one who can't do things for her. Don't I already have enough strikes against me?"

He looks down at my file, which I find amusing for some reason. "Well, let's see, you're an athlete, a good student, you have friends, people like you, you're handsome. Yes, I can see why you think you have so many strikes against you."

"I mean … it isn't really like that. She's just … I've been wanting to talk to her for a year and now she asks me out. I wish it would have happened before all of this. Before I was this," I say, pointing to my chest.

For the first time he looks at me like I would have expected a shrink to. Like he's tapped into some font of wisdom that I couldn't possibly be aware of. "Cal, I'd strongly suggest that you talk to her and tell her how you feel. She doesn't sound like she'll be scared off. But in the meantime, let me ask you a question. Okay?"

I wait to see what he's going to pull out this time but his words surprise me. "You're playing ball and you're down two runs in the third. The bases are loaded, there are two out, and you're up. And you strike out and that stinks, right?"

"Definitely," I say, shocked that we're talking about ball.

"So now it's the bottom of the ninth and you're still down the same two runs and there are men at first and third. You slam it over the wall. Your team wins."

"Okay…"

"It still stinks that you struck out the first time. But it doesn't take away the fact that you won the game at the end of the day. Right?"

I cough out a laugh. "You're saying that it's better late than never?"

"In your case, I'm actually saying that later *is* better. Because I'm not sure you would have let yourself explore this opportunity before. I suspect that you would have stood at the plate and watched strike three go right by you."

It's strange, but he just might be right. I don't know how I would have reacted had Ally and I talked before. Could I have made the time? What would I have done if Lizzie had needed me? Now I've got the time to see where this can go. And although I still don't know how I'm going to get behind the wheel of a car with her in it, I at least leave the office wanting to try.

And once again, I completely forget about the yellow list in my back pocket.

TWENTY

On Saturday morning, Spencer comes over to get me. I've hardly slept, but that's okay. I'm tired in that vague way that makes it hard to be too upset or worried about anything and I'm hoping that will work in my favor.

I drop him off at home on the way to the hospital with promises that Sweeney will survive. That I'll observe speed limits. That no food or drink will cross the threshold of its door. That I'll get the car washed if we go through any mud.

Surprisingly, it's easier to drive alone. Without Spencer in the car, without anyone, the only one I have to worry about hurting is myself. I wouldn't say I'm comfortable, but at least I'm moving.

My appointment at the hospital goes well. There are no words for how happy I am that I'll only be having biopsies once a month now. I guess it shows because three different nurses comment on how cheerful I seem, and I am, just not only for the reason they think.

I'm not quite as calm driving to Ally's house. She lives in a really high-end subdivision where each house is different. Some have columns, some have fountains out front. We have a nice house, but these are in a different league altogether. The closer I get, the more anxious I feel. I almost forget that in the middle of the day is a baseball game. That says something on its own.

I'm a little early so I have the luxury of parking down the block from Ally's house and taking a few minutes to calm down. I do all of the usual deep breathing things, counting backwards from a hundred, running through the batting averages of the players who are going to be starting today, that sort of thing. By the time I finally pull up in her drive I don't think I look red and sweaty like someone who has just run a marathon, or worse, like someone who had to sit in a borrowed car down the block to calm down.

She must be waiting by the door because she comes running out as soon as I pull up. She's wearing jeans and a Mustangs T-shirt, the same thing half the people at the game today will be wearing, but there's no chance of anyone looking as good in them as she does. Lizzie wolf-whistles in my head. I'm eternally grateful that Ally can't hear her.

Ally smiles wide when she sees me and gets in the car. Without a pause, she leans over and gives me a quick hug that makes all the hair on the back of my neck stand up. She smells like vanilla and sunshine.

"Thanks for picking me up," she says. "I would have hated to miss this game."

"Any time." I mean it as much as someone who hasn't been able to drive can mean something like that.

I watch as she puts on her seat belt and then I take a deep breath and back the car out of her drive. The trip to Fairview involves a short stint on the freeway that I'm really dreading, but I'm hoping that sitting next to Ally will distract me.

Already, though, my hands are clammy on the wheel

and I can feel an all-too-familiar pounding start in my temples in spite of the fact that we're only doing twenty-five down her street. I'm still worried that I'm not safe to drive with; that what happened with Lizzie will happen again.

My thoughts, not even Lizzie's, are so loud that I'm not talking to Ally and she's looking ahead, not talking to me. I'm sure by now she's figured out that I'm a nutcase and she regrets ever asking me to come get her.

As we turn the corner onto the street that will lead us towards the highway, she says, "Can I ask you for a favor?"

"Sure," I push out through my clenched teeth.

"I know it sounds funny, but my dad said he might buy me a new car for senior year and I was thinking of getting one of these. A Golf, I mean. I've never been behind the wheel of one, though. Do you think Spencer would mind if I were the one to drive us there?"

I pull over and pry my hands off the steering wheel one finger at a time. I know it's bullshit, and she knows it's bullshit, but still, she's throwing me this lifeline and making it look so effortless. I don't know what I've done to deserve her being so nice to me.

I say a quick prayer that Spencer won't kill me, unbuckle the seat belt, and get out. She does the same and then we've switched places and are ready to go.

She puts the car into drive and soon we're calmly heading down the road. I'm surprised to see her turning the opposite way from the freeway. "I promise I'll give the car back to you after the game, but I thought we'd take the side roads. You know, in case you wanted to come back this way."

I turn on the radio and find that Spencer left it on my favorite local rock station. Big surprise. He hasn't missed a trick.

But that gets me thinking. This is all too good, too easy. What the hell am I doing in this car with Ally Martin driving me around like I'm her boyfriend or something? It doesn't make sense after our silent staring contest. Did Dillard set me up somehow? That idea starts to fester inside me and it only take a few blocks before I'm worried I might be sick if I don't get some answers. The cold sweat is pouring out of me already.

"Pull over, Ally. Please, can you pull over now?"

She doesn't hesitate. She swings the car over to the edge of a playground that reminds me far too much of the one at the monastery where Lizzie and I used to hang out.

Once we've stopped she gives me a concerned look, like she's worried I'm going to pass out or die. I'm getting sick of people looking at me like that.

"What is it? Are you sick? Are you okay?"

"I'm … yeah, I think so. Okay, I mean," I say, and I realize that the feeling like I'm going to puke all over the car has subsided and I can mostly breathe again. "Ally, what's this all about?"

"This?"

"You and me. Why are we here? I know your car is in the shop and all, but there are a million people you could have asked for a ride today and any of the guys would have jumped at the chance. You know that Dillard would have loved to drive you." I throw the joke in hoping that the rest of what I'm saying doesn't come across as too freaky.

"I'll pretend that you don't sound like you're regretting being here with me," she says and unbuckles her seat belt.

"Shit, I'm sorry. That wasn't what I meant."

"I know." She smiles again and my stomach lurches, but not in a bad way. "Come on." She gets out of the car and I've got no choice but to follow. She starts to head for the swings, but I just can't do it. It reminds me too much of Lizzie. I grab Ally's hand and lead her over to the old metal merry-go-round. We sit down, both in the same space so that we aren't separated by one of the metal bars. I focus on the trees over-head rather than the fact that I'm actually holding hands with this girl because I know the sheer reality of it would freak me out, but she hasn't let go and I don't want to.

We sit there like that for a minute, both of us look-ing around the surprisingly empty playground, before she starts talking.

"You know, ever since I transferred to Maple Grove you've been watching me," she says.

I feel my face go red and wonder if the next words out of her mouth will include the words "restraining order."

She holds up her other hand to keep me from saying anything. "I know that you've been watching me because I've been watching you too. But what I never understood is why you've never ever, in over a year, come over to talk to me."

"Ally, I . . . " Abject terror somehow isn't going to be a valid explanation and beyond that I have nothing more rational to offer without spilling all of Lizzie's secrets. Thankfully, she put her hand on my arm and stops me.

"I know I'm guilty too." She looks at me shyly through

her dark lashes. "I mean, I wanted to talk to you, but I just heard so much about 'Cal Ryan baseball star.' My dad never stops talking about you. Plus..." She stops and all of a sudden she isn't looking at me. "I heard all the rumors. You know...about the three of you."

I'll bet she did.

I can tell from her expression that she didn't want to cop to it, but I sigh because it makes my stomach sort of twist to think of her hearing those things.

"Did you believe them?" My voice comes out a little shaky. The last thing I really want to do is to have to discuss each of the rumors with her, dissecting my life like a lab rat.

To her credit, she looks right at me and gives me what is probably the most honest answer she could have. "I don't know. I mean, I guess I didn't know what to believe. I just heard them whenever your name came up." She puts her other hand on top of mine and brings it to sit on her raised knees. "And Spencer and Lizzie..."

"What?"

"They kind of scared me," she admits. It's so strange because the Ally that lives in my head isn't afraid of anything or anyone. I guess I didn't know as much about her as I thought.

"Why?"

"Well, Spencer is just Spencer. I mean, I keep waiting for him to turn out to be a jerk or something. Can anyone really be that nice?"

Her question breaks the tension a little and makes me laugh.

"Yeah, he's an alien, don't worry about it."

She nods like she's really contemplating that Spencer might be from another planet.

"I'm kidding," I say, squeezing her hand. "He's just a really good guy. We've been friends almost as long as I can remember."

"Cool," she says like she's letting out a breath. "And Lizzie. She seemed like she didn't really care what anyone thought. And the three of you looked like you never needed anyone else. Like you were this complete package. So I figured … you know … maybe you just weren't interested."

I think I would have liked her, Cal. Don't fuck this up.

The combination of Ally's and Lizzie's words make my head spin a little. They're both just … right.

"Yeah," I say to say something. Even though all of the rumors weren't true, Ally isn't really wrong about us. What she didn't know was that, ever since she came to Maple Grove, there had been three compartments to my life: baseball, my best friends Spencer and Lizzie, and this space where I wanted her to be. I open my mouth to tell her, but she keeps talking.

"Then, I joined drama club this semester and got to know Spencer a little bit, and you and I got thrown together on the team, and … " She squeezes my hand, really hard. "Spencer and I started talking one day…" She winces and a guilty look crosses her face as she tugs on her sleeve. I'm worried that whatever she's about to say is going to ruin this wonderful thing that hasn't even had a chance to get started. "I asked him about you."

"Why?" I ask, shocked.

She looks exasperated for the first time. "You really don't get it, do you? I've been to your games. I've been waiting for you to talk to me, but you never did. You were watching me every time I looked over. Every single time for over a year."

Ha! Told you!

I suddenly feel like a total idiot. All of those nights that I'd spent in my room alone dreaming of this girl before I even knew that she's as great as she is and she was sitting in her own room wondering why I was being such a dork. All those times that Lizzie said that I should talk to her and I didn't listen because it was Lizzie and I wasn't ever totally sure what her motivation was, I was dropping the ball. All that wasted time and it's one more thing that's all my fault.

I kick off the merry-go-round until we're spinning around slowly. I try to watch the trees go by, the street, the rest of the playground, but I can't keep myself from looking into Ally's gray eyes. I want to respond, to apologize, to do something, but I'm in over my head and so I grasp at something completely different. Something that is suddenly crystal clear. This was a set-up, but it had nothing to do with Justin Dillard at all.

"What did Spencer tell you? He told you that I was having problems driving, didn't he? This is all his doing."

She grabs my hand again and links our fingers together and smiles like she's proud of herself. "It wasn't total bullshit. I did need a ride. And Spencer thought it would solve both problems. It would get you behind the wheel and it would force you to have a real conversation with me."

Well, that explains why he was willing to let me drive

his precious car. A slow blush creeps up her face and while I'm processing the fact that my best friend was behind this whole thing she says, "He told me other things too."

Crap. I can't believe there's more. "Like what?" I try to imagine Ally and Spencer sitting in a room talking about me and what he might have told her, but I come up short. And I don't want to get it wrong. I don't want to tell her something that she won't like, that will ruin this magic.

"Well, for instance, he said that you like things to be planned in advance."

I relax a little at this because it's true and I find it interesting that, out of everything, that's what Spencer thought was so important.

"Yeah," I admit. "I'm not really big on surprises."

She nods and folds her arms. There's something practical and businesslike in her gesture. "Fine. Just so you know. After the game, when we get back, I'm planning to kiss you. I wanted you to know that. I mean, if that's okay with you."

For a minute I assume she's joking. I mean, how often does it happen that reality is better than what you dream about? But no, her face is deadly serious. And there's something flickering within me, something pushing me forward, perhaps it's Lizzie, perhaps it's years of pent-up desire. Whatever it is, I give in to it because I've spent enough time being an idiot for one lifetime.

I swing for the fences and lean in to kiss her.

As good as it was to kiss her in my dreams, this is in another league altogether. Time stops. The entire world holds its breath and there isn't a single sensible thought going through my head and for once, I don't care.

Somewhere under all of that, I can't help but think about the only kiss I can compare this to, the one with Spencer. But I push that thought out of my head with everything I have as soon as I realize it's there.

When we come up for air, she says "wow" and smiles. "I'd say that was worth waiting for. I really don't want to wait another year for the next one, though."

I put my arm around her. I know it won't last after we get in the car and leave, but for this one moment in time, I feel like there are no rules, no barriers between us. "I'm sorry, Ally," I say because I'm not sure what else I can give her in way of explanation.

She pulls back and for a second I see the hurt in her eyes. "For kissing me?"

"No, damn, no. I'm definitely not sorry for that." I watch her face relax. "I just, I don't know how to explain it to you. It wasn't you. It was never you. I was just scared, and Spencer and I were spending so much time trying to keep Lizzie together and ... " I shrug. "I don't really have an excuse. Other than that I'm an idiot."

She leans in and holds my eyes with hers, like she's trying to make a decision. Then she runs her hand through my hair, sending shivers all the way through me before kissing me on the lips as gentle as feather. "Yeah, you are. But I think I might give you the chance to redeem yourself."

Her words and the kiss make me dizzy and I have to lean back against the metal bar to steady myself. What I'm feeling reminds me of when I hit the grand slam to win the series last year. It was the home run that cemented my place on the varsity team and I thought that was the best thing that had ever happened to me.

But something about this moment feels better. And I may not understand why it's happening, but she's right that I'm not dumb enough to make the same mistake twice so I'm not questioning anything.

Instead, I tell her what Dr. Reynolds told me about how hitting a home run in the ninth inning is just as good, and sometimes better, than doing it earlier so long as you win in the end.

She laughs again. "That's a low blow using a baseball analogy. I'm not sure I can be mad at you for not talking to me sooner if you're going to do that."

"Good," I say and close my eyes. I feel the craziest mix of emotions: mine, which basically boil down to amazement, layered on top of Lizzie's, who is gloating like nobody's business.

For a minute I panic and wonder if maybe I'm making this all up. Maybe my screwed-up head has taken things to a new level.

But then I open my eyes again and feel her hand, gentle as her kiss, barely touching the fabric of my shirt right over my scar.

"Are you okay?" she asks and I don't know if she means right now at this moment or in a bigger way.

I look up into her eyes. It's an amazing thing to look at her and not feel like I have to look away before I get caught.

"Yeah, I'm fine." I put my hand over hers and press it gently over where my scar is. It feels like she's knitting things together, which I know isn't true, but we're this circuit of energy in that moment: me, and Ally, and Lizzie. I feel like I could run a marathon, but don't want to move a muscle.

"Does it hurt?" she asks softly.

I pull her hand down and wrap my other one around it. "The scar is sore, but other than that..." I almost tell her about Lizzie, but stop myself. Forgiving me for staring at her is one thing; telling her that Lizzie is somehow still calling some of the shots is something I'm not ready to risk. "I don't think anything could hurt me right now."

She smiles and I wonder if it will always be so easy to make her smile. She leans over and her lips brush my cheek. "I hate to do this, but I think we're going to be late to the game."

I look at my watch and realize she's right. "How fast can you drive?" I ask.

"Fast enough." She smiles and pulls both of us off the merry-go-round and back towards the car, where she gets into the driver's seat without even asking.

Ally wasn't lying. She gets us to the field in plenty of time without breaking too many laws along the way. Coach Byrne gives me a funny look as Ally and I walk up together. Not a bad one, just one that says he knows something he didn't know before.

I take my place at his side while Ally climbs up the stairs to the concrete bunker behind home plate where she'll watch the game alongside Fairview's scorekeeper. I turn and realize that Coach is staring at me with a smirk on his face.

"Who's starting at first?" I ask, preoccupied.

Coach laughs. "Good, Ryan. Wasn't sure you remembered we were playing baseball today." He glances appreciatively at the bunker where somewhere inside Ally is setting up for the game. My face goes seven shades of red as he claps me on the back and laughs.

TWENTY-ONE

We only lose by two runs, and Dillard commits an error so it's a good day. A great day.

Coach Byrne said he suspected we weren't going to win but, because of the error, he's making Dillard go with him when he mows his brother's three-acre yard, which is his payment for losing the bet on the game. I have fantasies of that jerk being eaten by a carnivorous lawn mower.

As we all stand around afterwards, waiting for Coach to dismiss us, Ally comes over and puts her hand on my shoulder. It isn't anything crazy; I mean, she isn't mauling me or anything. But the way she puts that one hand on me makes it clear we're together and for a minute, transplant or no transplant, every single guy on that team wants to be me. Coach actually winks at me as we head to the car and I have to stop again and wonder at my luck.

Neither of us is really hungry, but Ally and I had planned on eating, so she drives us to pick up some sandwiches and we pull back into the playground. We sit and talk as the day-light fades. After everything that's been going on, after not talking to Ally for so long, it feels wonderful to be discussing silly things, our favorite teachers, vacations we took as kids, what we like to read.

I tell her that I always read the end of a book first. She tells me that she joined the softball team in junior high because she knew her dad wanted a kid who played sports, but she wasn't very good at it and settled on scorekeeping.

I tell her that I'm not a fan of the dark and she counters with the fact that she thinks she might want to go into psychology.

I tell her that I'm going to study meteorology, and she tells me that she's terrified of spiders.

It starts to get dark and I don't want to go home. Ally says she doesn't either. The metal equipment around the playground is cold so we climb up on top of one of the picnic tables. I lie down on my back with Ally next to me, holding onto the edge with one hand and me with the other.

After all of the talking is done, we're quiet. Not like we've been this past year, afraid to talk to each other. This is a different type of quiet. It's soft, like a blanket that's wrapped around us.

She puts her head on my chest, just to the side of my scar. It feels strange to have the weight of her head there and it pulls the skin near my incision a little, making it tingle. I can smell her shampoo and her long hair tickles my neck.

"I can hear your heartbeat," she says.

I'm sure she can, because it feels like a marching band is about to jump out of my chest. I feel like I'm on fire.

But still I have to stop myself before I tell her that it isn't my heart. She knows about the accident and all, but if she doesn't know already, I'm not going to point out what a freak I really am. So instead I bite my lip and stay quiet, trying to focus on every place on my body that she's touching and trying to count the stars to stay calm.

It's a crazy clear night actually and the sky looks like it's lit up just for us.

"Make a wish," she says.

I slowly roll out from under her and over onto my side so that I'm facing her, trying not to pull the skin on my chest even more.

"You do that?" I ask her in amazement.

"Doesn't everyone?"

I think back to that last time Lizzie called me and the night we spent out in the playground. "Some people don't believe in wishes."

For some people they never come true.

"That's sad," she says, sitting up on her elbows. "But you do, right?"

"Yeah, I believe in wishes," I say. Even though I know that there are important things I should be wishing for, like health and stuff, there is only one thing I want to wish for, but I think it's coming true right now.

It must be clear on my face because her eyes shine as she lays her hand back gently on my chest.

"So what are you wishing for?" she asks.

"This," I say and lean up to kiss her.

———

She offers to drive home and I let her. We roll the windows down and the breeze coming through is the only sound until she says, "Relax, Cal," and reaches over to take my hand. I look down and realize that I've been curling and uncurling the scorecard from the game so that it looks like a tube that's been run over by a truck.

"I'm fine," I say, but as the words come out of my mouth I try to figure out what it is that's suddenly making me feel so anxious. Then it hits me. "So, what's going to happen on Monday?"

To her credit, not only does she understand what I'm asking, but she doesn't laugh at me. Most girls would have, I think. Lizzie would have. But Ally just smiles and squeezes my hand like it's a question she's been expecting.

In the voice of a teacher talking to either a very young or a very stupid student, she says, "On Monday, we will both go to school. And you will not stare at me without talking to me. And I will not stare at you without talking to you, okay?"

"Okay," I say. It sounds so easy when she puts it that way, but she isn't done.

"In fact, Spencer has rehearsal at lunch on Monday and I don't have to go in to read lines until later in the week. So unless you already have plans or don't want to, I was thinking that maybe we could have lunch together. You know, actually spend time with each other in public like real people?"

I can feel my cheeks get hot and I want to apologize again, but I don't. She knows I'm sorry and I deserve the hard time she's giving me. So instead I try to say something normal. Something that Spencer might say. "Lunch sounds good."

"It's a date then."

Date. The word bounces around my brain like a pin-ball in a machine, ricocheting off all the dusty and unused corners. Of course I know that Maple Grove's lunchroom doesn't constitute a real date. But it's a darn good start. In my head a round of slow, sarcastic applause begins and I'm glad that Ally's concentrating on driving and doesn't see my smile.

The drive is way shorter going home than it was on the way to Ally's. When we pull up to her house, the porch light is on and I can see her dad moving behind the sheer curtains.

I don't want to get out of the car, but when she goes to open the door I fly around and open it for her.

"A gentleman. I like that," she says with a flirtatious glint in her eyes that lights a fire in me I can feel down to my toes.

"Thanks," I say. "I mean, for the … " and then I stop. I was going to say "for the ride," but that's stupid since even though she did the work, I was meant to be driving her. So I shrug and say, "I had fun."

"I did too," she says. I stand by the car watching until she goes inside and waves at me through the window.

The drive back is easy because I'm not thinking about driving. *At all.*

The first thing I do when I get in the house is pull out my now-crumpled piece of yellow paper and add #11 to my Ally list: *She's a really, REALLY good kisser.* And then I underline #10: *I think it might be easy to fall in love with her* four or five times.

The next thing I do is to call Spencer, who answers on the first ring.

"Thanks for the car." I can picture him sitting in the black armchair in his room, his legs draped over the side, a book in one hand and his phone in the other waiting for me to call and tell him that both me and Sweeney made it back. "I'll get it back to you tomorrow."

He laughs. "Is it in one piece?"

"Very funny. Yes, it's fine," I answer, neglecting to tell him that Ally did most of the driving.

"Are you in one piece?" he asks more cautiously.

"I'm..." I pause long enough that Spencer finishes the sentence for me

"Speechless? Smitten? Besotted?"

Sometimes it's hard when you have friends who know you so well that they can read the meaning behind every intonation in your voice. Sometimes, like now, it's the best thing in the world.

"Besotted?" I laugh. "Only you would say besotted."

"You aren't answering my question."

It's like that tree falling in a forest thing. If I don't tell Spencer something, if I keep it to myself, anything can happen. I can wake up and it will have gone away. I can change my mind and it won't matter. It isn't real until he's heard it.

So answering his question is a commitment to swinging at the ball. Once I'm in, I'm in. I hesitate but only for a second. I want this to be real. "Yes, Yeats, I'm besotted."

"About time," he says. "You can thank me later."

"Is this..." I start, trying to choose the right words. "I mean, you and Rob... I can't imagine feeling like this and not..." I'm mangling the question, but, as usual, he gets it.

"Yeah," he says and then there's silence.

"What?"

"Cal, you and Ally aren't two thousand miles away

from each other. And Rob hasn't even told his parents that he's gay. I don't want to be anyone's secret. It's just … complicated." Spencer sounds sad and I wish he'd go for the thing with Rob even though I'm the last one to talk.

"But there's email, and webcams, and I've heard they've got these metal birds that fly called planes, and … maybe you can help him?" I think of all the times that Spencer pushed me to talk to Ally. I guess it's always hardest to take your own advice.

I can hear his smile on the other end of the phone. "Yeah, mister expert, I get it. I'm … working on it."

When I hang up the phone, I send Ally a text.

Is it odd that I feel I know you so well when we haven't talked that much?

I don't use typical text abbreviations because Lizzie never texted and Spencer is a word snob. Text speak is one of the few things that sets him on edge so I'm just out of the habit.

After I send it, I head downstairs and take my evening meds right on time. It takes about ten very long minutes but then my phone chirps and Ally's name pop up.

We've talked a lot. Just not with words.

I wonder, for a minute, if all of the stars I've wished on have had a conference and decided to band together to make this possible. I don't know how it's possible that she's forgiven me for so many things, when I can't forgive myself.

TWENTY-TWO

"So you've asked Ally out, right?" Spencer is sitting on the floor of my room rolling a baseball back and forth between his hands. We're supposed to be studying for a chem test, but neither of us is having much luck focusing on it.

"I'm having lunch with her on Mondays," I answer. "It's kind of a thing now."

"It's a *thing*? What does that even mean?" Spencer picks up the ball, my phone, and a stapler and starts to juggle them. It's kind of hypnotic.

"It's the only time you and the play aren't monopolizing her. She doesn't have rehearsals on Mondays. So we have lunch."

"In the school cafeteria? Wow, that's romantic." Spencer catches the ball and sets it down, followed by the stapler. When he catches my phone, he stares at it. "Call her," he says, holding it out to me.

"Why?"

Spencer tosses the phone and it lands near me on the bed. Then he lies back until he's flat on the floor looking up at my stars. "It's your turn. She started your lunch 'thing.' Now you need to move forward or you're just going to get stuck in a rut."

Something in his voice, the way he's lying stretched and tense, makes me wonder if he's really talking about me and Ally at all.

Do it. You have nothing to lose. Have some balls for a change.

For once, I kind of agree with Lizzie. After that first week, Ally and I have had lunch together for the last couple of Mondays and we've been hanging out at practice. I'm pretty sure she'd say "yes" if I asked her to do something else. So I grab the phone and call her.

"Hey Ally," I say to her voicemail. "It's me. Cal." I think fast. "My parents are going to some foundation dinner tonight and I was wondering if you wanted to come over and grab a pizza or something."

I glance at Spencer, who is leaning forward on his elbows and staring at me with his eyes wide open. He never thought I'd go through with it. "Pizza?" he mouths at the same time that Lizzie says it in my head. I know it isn't the healthiest option or the most romantic one, but they've obviously forgotten that I can't cook.

"Or something," I repeat. "Anyhow...give me a call. Later. Okay, bye."

I disconnect the call and throw my phone back to Spencer. "Your turn."

"My turn what?"

"Call Rob," I say. For some reason the whole thing reminds me of Lizzie's truth or dare games.

Spencer goes a little pale and bolts straight up. "No, I don't think so." He picks up his chem book and starts riffling through it, but I can tell he isn't really looking at it. He sighs as he puts it back down. "I've been thinking a lot since..." He closes his eyes and take a breath so deep I can see his black T-shirt rise. "Losing Lizzie..." He stops again.

I hang off the end of my bed. It freaks me out when Spencer starts to sound unsure of things. I move to the floor and sit down next to him. My chest hums. Lizzie always gets like that when I'm close to Spencer and *that* freaks me out enough that I move back to sit on the bed.

Spencer gives me a suspicious look, puts my phone back on the edge of the bed, and stares at it. "*Carpe Diem.* Seize the day. Who knows if we'll even be here tomorrow? I get it. But Rob and I aren't even in the same time zone. We have video chats and it's good. Really good. Just like last summer. But only when his dad isn't home because his dad would kill him if he knew he was gay. So really I'm just wasting my time, right?"

I try to remember the last time Spencer needed my advice on something. I wish it were about fielding a line-drive, or plotting a star chart, because relationships are probably what I'm most clueless about.

I think about what he said in The Cave about his night with Lizzie. And how he felt about her and wished he could be different. I know that I need to reassure him. Spencer is usually happy but there was something different about him when Rob was around. Like he was both extra happy and kind of sad at the same time. It all felt very big and important. Life changing.

"Lizzie would tell you to call him," I say although my head is surprisingly silent.

"You think?" he asks. "She was kind of on the fence where Rob was concerned."

"I'm not sure that had anything to do with Rob." The

dull throbbing in my temples tells me that I'm right on the mark. "But you should anyhow."

Spencer says, "I'll think about it," and I suspect that's as far as we're going to get today.

He reaches over, grabs his bag, and stares at me with the concerned Spencer Yeats look I've come to know too well lately.

"What?"

"Don't freak out," he orders.

I take a deep breath. The last time Spencer started a sentence that way, he told me that his parents had offered to pull him out of Maple Grove and send him to a private arts school.

I lower myself back down to the floor, careful to keep enough distance that Lizzie doesn't start up.

He rummages around in his bag, pulls out his tablet, and turns it on.

"He died," he says, looking down at the screen.

"Who?"

"Martin Fuller," he answers.

I try to place the name, thinking of Spencer's family members. His favorite band. Other kids at school. "Um."

He holds the tablet out to me, but then pulls it back against his chest.

"He's the guy who hit us," Spencer says. And when I don't answer, he says, "The driver . . ."

"Stop." I know who he's talking about. I've done everything I can to avoid knowing his name or anything about him. *Martin Fuller.* Now I have to live with knowing that.

"I think you should read this." Spencer holds the tablet out towards me again.

"Why?" The computer hangs in the air between us until Spencer's arm waivers and he puts it down on the floor.

"Because he's done it before. Not killed anybody. But he hit a biker and ran his car into a ravine a couple of years ago while he was on the phone."

I pull myself up and go to the window. It rained overnight, but now it's stopped and I really should go for a run. I'm used to a lot of exercise, but I'm not used to being tired all the time and not having games to get ready for makes me realize that exercise for exercise's sake is just boring.

"Cal?"

"What?" I ask without turning around.

Spencer comes up next to me and we stand, side by side, watching it not rain. Watching nothing.

"Stop beating yourself up. It was this guy's fault and now he's dead."

I've heard my parents discussing some lawsuit against the driver's estate, but they change the subject when I come into the room. I wonder if this will make them happy or if it will be harder to collect, because that's what they seem to care most about.

"I've been thinking about going to see Lizzie's mother," I say, which really isn't changing the subject at all.

Spencer reaches up to put a hand on my arm and then takes it back. This is our punishment for what happened that night in The Cave. I hate that we've both gotten so nervous about touching each other.

"I get why you think you should," Spencer says. "But I also think you're going to regret it."

I nod. He's right as always, but I've been thinking about it a lot. "She's a bitch, but she was still Lizzie's mom."

Just thinking about going over there makes my chest feel tight. Lizzie's mom is about the last person in the world I want to see, but I just don't know how I'm going to be able to live with myself otherwise. I certainly don't deserve to take the easy way out.

"You want me to go with you?" he asks.

The idea of having Spencer with me makes my chest ease up. But I think I need to do this one without a baby-sitter. "Nah, I'll be fine," I say.

I'm sure Spencer knows that I don't really believe it. But like the best friend he is, he just nods and says, "Of course you will."

After Spencer leaves, I go before I chicken out and by the time I get to Lizzie's house, I'm sticky with sweat and starting to convince myself that maybe this wasn't the right decision. After all, how could I possibly apologize? What words do I have that could make up for Lizzie being dead?

And it isn't just the accident either. Had her mother not agreed to let the doctors use Lizzie's heart, I'd be dead too. How the hell do I thank her for giving me her daughter's heart?

I make it as far as the end of her block and stop. It wasn't like I'd expected much to have changed. It isn't like the bricks of her house know that Lizzie is gone, not like the trees are missing her as much as I do.

On the other hand, it's impossible to imagine that things could continue the way they were. I mean, her mom was a nasty drunk who was never there when Lizzie needed her, but now that Lizzie is gone, I can't imagine her not realizing what she's lost.

I expect her mom to really let me have it and I deserve whatever she's going to dish out, but for some reason that doesn't make it any easier. I've never heard a story about Lizzie's mom that made me believe that she's the type to forgive. I don't imagine that I'm going to be part of one now.

Don't do this, Cal. You don't have to do this.

"Shut up, Lizzie," I say without thinking. Thankfully, it's a quiet Sunday and aside from a huge Appliance Depot truck, the block is deserted so no one can see me talking to myself, but it's really not a habit I want to get into.

Spence's right. This isn't going to go well. Trust me this one time.

I start walking, as much to avoid Lizzie's voice as anything, although I know she's along for the ride.

As I get up closer to the truck, I realize it's parked in front of Lizzie's house. Two guys with muscles in their arms that look like sides of beef are wrestling a stainless steel dishwasher out of the back by the time I reach the house.

I stand and stare because Lizzie's mom never had money for anything like this. She sometimes barely had money for food and clothes. Lizzie was ace at turning thrift store finds into something she could wear, but her mom was certainly no help.

I'm frozen, so still that I don't notice one of the guys

almost bump into me and I have to step back. Just as I do, Lizzie's mom comes out of the house. She's wearing one of those gauzy housecoat things that my mom wouldn't be caught dead in and smoking a cigarette.

When she notices me, she says, "You here to lend these boys a hand?" and points to the guys on the truck.

"Um…" I spit out, my brain a tangle of nonsense words.

"Be careful with those," she yells as the guys strain to lift a huge marble slab down from the truck. "I'm redoing the kitchen," she says in my direction, as if that's the only thing on her mind.

It's been a while since I've seen Mrs. McDonald, I know, but still I assume that she has to know who I am. Then again, maybe all that alcohol has done something to her brain.

"Mrs. McDonald, it's Cal," I say, bracing myself for her reaction. "I'm Cal."

"I know who you are," she snaps. "Do you think I've lost my mind?"

She looks into the truck like a kid exploring their Christmas presents. I almost expect her to climb in and peek under the package's wrapping.

I take a deep breath. "Mrs. McDonald, I just want to tell you how sorry I am about Lizzie. I really, really miss her and I know this must be so hard on you too."

My words make her turn and stare at me like I've said something stupid. Something about that makes me want to cry, but I blink and spit out the rest of my useless speech. "Thank you for signing those papers. For her heart, I mean."

I wish she'd say something but she just stands there

with her eyes squinted like she's waiting for something else. I don't know what words she wants to hear.

"You came all the way over here to say that?"

"Yeah." I gulp. My throat feels raw, like I've been swallowing glass. I search her face to see some sign of Lizzie in it, but there's nothing. No sign at all of them being related.

"You could have called," she says. "Not like she was going to be able to use the heart where she is. And when your friend offered me that check, well, I'm not stupid."

Lizzie's heart starts hammering uncomfortably fast and I'm aware that what had been a sheen of sweat on my forehead has become a river of stress-induced liquid adrenaline. I try to wipe it away with the sleeve of my shirt, but it doesn't make much of a difference.

Spencer gave her money. Of course he did.

Lizzie's mom glances at the house and looks thoughtful. I hope she's going to say something about remembering Lizzie, or that she'll get mad at me or do something that makes sense.

"This whole kitchen thing…" she says. "It's from the insurance money. I figured that it's fitting. I mean, that was her job here anyhow. Keeping the kitchen clean and running."

It's just too much. My vision narrows until all I can see is Lizzie's mom. Everything else is fuzzy around the edges and I feel dizzy, like the ground suddenly isn't solid anymore.

I stumble down to my knees on the grass and vomit up everything I've eaten in the last day.

When I'm done and my head clears a little, Mrs. McDonald looks from me to the mess I've made on her lawn. "Well," she says. "Good thing we're expecting more rain."

I feel like shit, but my head is quiet. To her credit, Lizzie doesn't say "I told you so."

TWENTY-THREE

I consider calling Ally and telling her that I'm tired and might have food poisoning and need to cancel dinner. The way I feel after seeing Lizzie's mom, it isn't stretching the truth.

But something about watching my parents put on their best "we're pillars of the community" clothes and get ready to go to their charity dinner makes me not want to be alone. And besides, this is Ally. I may feel like crap, but I'm not stupid enough to cancel plans with her.

She's right on time, which is great except that I fell asleep on the couch and have pillow lines impressed into the right side of my face when I get up to answer the door.

She smiles when she points it out. "You look cute this way," she says. "Like a little boy."

I duck into the half-bath downstairs and splash some water on my face. I'll take the "cute" but I'm not sure how I feel about the "little boy" comment.

We order pizza and as we're eating, I tell her about my visit to Lizzie's mom.

"At least you did what you felt was right," Ally says.

I eat the pepperoni off an extra slice. The grease might just be the best thing I've tasted since the accident. "Yeah, but Spencer warned me it would be a bust. I don't know why I thought Lizzie's mom would have changed."

Ally picks at the salad we got as a side to at least fool ourselves into believing we were eating something healthy.

"I still think you're brave to have gone over there. And what happened would have changed most people, I think. When I was little, after my mom died, my dad and I moved in with my grandmother. One day I came home and found her in the garden with a potted petunia in her hand. She'd died. Just like that. In the garden."

The empty look on her face makes me shiver. "I'm sorry," I say. "That must have been hard."

Ally nods and puts her fork down. "We'd had a fight that morning. Well, I guess I was just being a brat. I was eight."

I begin to tell her that I'm sorry again, but something in her expression stops me.

"My dad told me that my grandmother had a heart condition and that she'd lived a good life and all. But it was hard. She had a twin sister I was very close to. My aunt Tilly. I kept wanting to say something, but I couldn't even look at her after that. I'm sure she thought I hated her."

"How come you couldn't talk to her?" I ask.

Ally looks up as if she's surprised by my question. "I just couldn't go through that again. I mean, what if Aunt Tilly died too? I felt like it was all my fault. All these people I loved dying. It felt easier just not to let myself be close to anyone."

Aside from Lizzie, no one close to me has ever died. Given how big a piece of me *she* took with her, I can't imagine how someone could survive losing so many people.

"Well, everyone dies eventually, right?" I choke out and instantly regret.

"Yeah, I just . . ." Finally Ally stops, as if she's suddenly realized who she's talking to. "Sorry. You probably think that's horrible of me. Let's just talk about something else."

223

I don't know if I think it's horrible, but I'm all for talking about something else. Thinking of Ally as some magnet for death doesn't exactly comfort me. She doesn't have to ask twice.

"Did you want to come upstairs to see the new telescope my parents got me? It's awesome. I can hook a camera up to it and you can see the planets. Even Pluto. I mean, I know that Pluto isn't really a planet anymore, but I think it should be and ... "

My nervous rambling works to change the subject, but it's her smile that shuts me up.

"Cal Ryan, are you inviting me up to your room?"

Lizzie laughs as I sputter, "Um. Yeah, but not like that, I mean ... "

Ally's smile brightens up her entire face. "Yes."

———————

The morning sun shines through the slats of the shade, sending lines all around the room that look like the just-mowed outfield grass on opening day.

I roll over and wallow in the vanilla smell on my pillow. Ally. Ally was here. Lying on my bed because we never quite made it to the window. Ally staring at the stick-on stars overhead while I pointed out constellations, explained retrograde, kissed her. Kissed her over and over and over again until I couldn't catch my breath and until it felt like we were melting together into some new kind of creature. Kissed her until the world went away.

I get out of bed with a smile on my face that not even the realization that I forgot to take my meds last night can change. I know enough not to double my morning dose and figure I'll call the doctor to see if I can pop by for a quick test this afternoon without my parents finding out. I've been perfect up until now, so I'm pretty sure missing that one dose isn't going to do anything major.

I head to school and between thinking about last night and having Monday lunch with Ally to look forward to, I'm parading from class to class with a rare stupid grin on my face. That is, until I see something that almost brings me to my knees.

I lean against a row of lockers to keep from collapsing. The blood rushes through my ears like the roar of a crowd. It's deafening and Lizzie is crying and wailing like I've never heard her before, not even when things with her mom were at their worst.

My hands are frozen into fists, the only fact keeping me from acting as I watch two of the janitorial crew repainting the inside of Lizzie's locker. Had I thought about it, I'd have known that they couldn't possibly leave her locker as it was. But at the same time, I can't bear to watch three years of her work, probably her best work, being scrubbed away.

Lizzie's paintings were usually dark and you could tell, from looking at what she was working on, how things were going at home. But this one painting, the one she kept locked behind a metal door where only she could see it, was inspiring and hopeful. Every time she added something to it, it seemed to take her one step closer to being happy in real life.

And now they're destroying it.

It feels like nothing more or less than them ripping Lizzie's heart out of my chest.

Stop them, Cal. Stop them.

Lizzie is screaming in my head and I seriously want to pull these workmen off of her locker and shove the paint-brushes they're holding down their throats. There's only a tiny kernel in the back of my brain that realizes they're just doing their job and I try to hold tight onto that little rational cell. But my ears are ringing from Lizzie's cries and I want to open my mouth and let her scream come out.

It feels like she's kicking her steel-toed boots against the sides of my head and it's all I can do to keep from doubling over in pain. I don't know what to do. Kids are streaming past me on their way to lunch or class. Everyone is pushing and shoving and laughing, but I don't move. I make them maneuver around me as I stand there like a statue, paying testament to Lizzie's every last brush stroke.

You can't let them do this. You can't...

Only when these guys are done, when they've made Lizzie's locker the same dull gray-brown as the other 1,402 in the school, and they've cleaned their brushes, and picked up their drop cloths, only then does it feel like it's possible for me to move my legs again.

Without thinking about anything except getting as far away as possible from the scene of this destruction, I head outside. The air feels cool on my face and only then do I realize that my face is wet with tears. Before I know it, I'm at the one place at the school that has always made me feel at home: the baseball field.

The ground is wet from the rain so I crawl into the dugout like a kid hiding under the covers in the middle of a nightmare. I know I'm alone, that no one has any reason to be coming to the diamond, so I let it out, all the emotion and pain I'm feeling. I let all of Lizzie's anger wash over me and fling a stack of bats, one by one, out into the field until my arm is so sore that I'm pretty sure I won't be able to lift it tomorrow.

My chest is starting to feel twisted, like someone is putting a vise around the muscles and turning it back and forth.

Cal. Cal. Cal.

My name rings through my head. It reminds me of that time that I got hit by a line drive and ended up with a concussion.

I try to slow my breathing, but fail. I always thought I had a high tolerance for pain, but I never had to worry about muscle strain killing me. *This* pain is freaking me out.

"Lizzie, I'm sorry. I'm really sorry." It's strange to be talking to her out loud, but my chest is really starting to hurt. "Stop. Please. They were just doing their job."

It was the only thing I had. The only thing I was good at. And you let them take it.

I sink down to the concrete floor and rub at my chest. My hands run across the raised edges of my scar. "I never wanted to hurt you, Lizzie. You know that. You fucking *know* that. I did everything I could."

I'm not sure I believe my own words. And when Lizzie whispers, *Well, it wasn't enough,* I realize what's happening. She and her heart are rejecting me.

TWENTY-FOUR

They put me in one of those little rooms in the ER that are meant for people who aren't staying overnight. I was here for a broken wrist once. And to get a tetanus shot after I stepped on a rusty rake that Justin Dillard "accidently" left outside my locker in sixth grade.

This time, Ben Evans found me in the dugout when he came to retrieve a batting glove he'd left behind. I told him to dial 911, but Coach was right behind him and said he'd drive me to the hospital. I ranted the whole way in the car. "Lizzie hates me. Her heart is rejecting me. I forgot my meds."

Coach sounded like he did when he came out to the mound to talk to our pitchers. "Breathe. You've got this. Focus." But I knew a pep talk wasn't going to help me.

I tuned him out and concentrated on keeping Lizzie's heart working, even though I could feel her fighting against me. It's funny how you can take breathing for granted: in, out, in, out. All day, without thinking. Now I had to work for every molecule of air. Now I had to fight Lizzie.

Coach left when my dad got there. Mom was in court and someone was sending her a message. I wonder if Spencer knew. Or if anyone had told Ally. I hope she didn't think I'd stood her up even though I did.

At some point between getting out of Coach Byrne's car and lying on the bed with oxygen going into my nose and a ridiculous hospital gown on and my father hovering over me, I realized that as much as I miss Lizzie, as horrible as I feel for what happened, I don't want to die too. For some reason, that comes as more of a surprise than I would have imagined. But now I know what I have to do.

"I need my phone," I say to Dad.

He rubs his temples like I'm asking to run a marathon. "You need to just relax, Cal. I'm sure someone will be here soon."

Lab techs come in and draw blood while nurses take my pressure and listen to my chest. The physical pain eased up after they gave me some shot, but the real pain of what I saw being done to Lizzie's locker is right in front of my eyes. And in my head.

"Can you get me some water?" My dad looks at me with a raised eyebrow, waiting for me to explain why really I just want him out of the room. "With ice."

"Cal, I think I should just stay here until the doctor comes."

I glare at him until he nods and leaves. I guess he figures I'm not going to die in the next five minutes and I hope it will take him longer than that to figure out where to go for a cup and then the water and ice. And a few minutes is just what I need.

"Lizzie. Come on. We have to talk about this." I close my eyes because I feel stupid looking at the wall and talking to an empty room.

At first there's just silence. A trickle of sweat down my forehead. The hiss of the oxygen being pumped into the tube in my nose.

I have nothing to say.

I smile through the pain. Just like Lizzie to break her silence to tell me she doesn't want to talk to me.

"Listen," I whisper. "I get it. I really do. I know what that painting meant to you."

Really? You think you do? Because Cal Ryan baseball star certainly had more than one thing in his life he was proud of.

I wince and don't remind her that I'll never play baseball again. "You had other things to be proud of." I realize as soon as the words are out of my mouth that they're going to set her off.

Yeah, I was barely hanging on in school. My mother hated me. And, oh yeah, I'm in love with my gay best friend. That's a lot to be proud of.

I don't call her out on her choice of present tense because her heart is beating all out of time inside me. Instead I take a deep breath and say, "You were a good person, Lizzie. A good friend. No one could ever make me laugh the way you did. The way you do. Still."

She's silent so I continue. "You're the only one I know who cared enough to sign up for the donor registry. You saved my life."

There's silence. So much silence. The type that seeps around corners and fills up empty spaces. For a minute I think that this is it. Lizzie's heart is going to stop beating. Then, in a small voice I've never heard her use, she says, *Don't fucking waste it.*

Before I can protest, my dad comes back into the room followed by the doctor and I brace myself for the bad news.

Spencer rustles up the stairs and into my bedroom, hidden under a bunch of bags.

I glance at him from the bed, where I'm propped up against a stack of pillows. "I'm surprised my parents let you up here. And what is all that?"

One by one he unloads his haul. "I brought you the stuff my mom used to give me when I was home sick from school." His stack of Archie comics and *Mad Libs* makes me laugh. I used to get them too. When I was eight. "And your homework from Mr. Brooks," he adds.

He acts like I'm home with a sore throat instead of the real reason, so I decide to cut to the chase. "I'm not dying, apparently."

He looks at me out of the corner of his eye. "I read that panic attacks are common among transplant recipients."

"Screwing up my meds last night probably didn't help either," I admit.

"Your dad told me about that. You never forget anything. What were you doing?" I don't have time to answer before the realization hits. "Shit. Ally was here last night, right?"

Last night, Ally, the stars, the way her hair looked against my pillow, they all flash back in a glorious instant. "Yeah, but ... I mean, we didn't ... "

"Have you talked to her today?" he asks, cutting me off.

"No. I was on my way to meet her, but ... did you see what they did to Lizzie's locker?"

I wait for Lizzie to say something, but my head is

quiet. "It really meant something to her," I continue. "And now it's gone."

Spencer nods. He knew what it meant as well as I did.

I hope he'll offer up some plan, some way to make things right. Instead he moves the comics over and sits down on the edge of the bed.

"I'm not sure how to say this, so I'm just going to dive in, okay?" As usual, Spencer doesn't wait for an answer. "I'm not going to pretend to know how you feel. I mean, a part of her is literally inside you. But she wouldn't want you making yourself miserable all the time."

I must still be under the effects of some of the meds because I burst out laughing. If Spencer only knew. I think, in some way, my feeling miserable is *exactly* what Lizzie wants.

But then maybe he does know, because he says, "You have to be alive to feel guilty. I've been thinking about that a lot lately. We're lucky to still be here. We're lucky to be here to feel *anything*."

"I know. I do. But…"

Spencer reaches over and puts his hand on my arm. This time I resist pulling away. "Cal, we're lucky. It doesn't always feel like it without Lizzie. But we are."

Suddenly, I'm very, very tired. "Fine. What do you want me to do?"

He sighs. I guess he thinks I'm just trying to play along, but I really am interested in what Spencer would do if he were me. "Go be happy with Ally. Study clouds and weather. Don't let yourself get stuck."

"Stuck" is actually a good word for me at the moment.

Maybe Spencer is right about moving forward, but that doesn't mean I know how to do it or how not to waste the chance, like Lizzie said. "Thanks for the comic books." I hope he'll read the rest of my meaning into those words.

"Any time," he says as he squeezes my arm and gets up. "Just one thing. Everyone at school is kind of fixated on you right now. First with … " Spencer stops, knowing that I don't want to hear the name. "With the driver dying. And now with you being carted off to the hospital. Just wanted you to be prepared for tomorrow."

Prepared. That one makes me laugh again.

TWENTY-FIVE

I left three messages and sent an email to Ally last night and never heard back, so my first goal at school is to find her. Spencer's pep talk, if that's what it was, has me a little energized. He's right in a way. I'm sad as hell about losing Lizzie, but when I was in so much pain yesterday and convinced that I was dying, I knew that I wanted to live. *Really* live.

I'm not sure what that looks like without baseball, but for the first time I at least want to figure it out.

I catch a glimpse of Ally in the hall, but so many people stop to ask me how I'm feeling that by the time I'm free, I've lost her.

When she never shows up to lunch, I know there's something wrong.

After school, I race through the halls hoping to make it to the auditorium before she gets there for rehearsal. My heart leaps when I see her, even though I expect her to either yell at me for standing her up yesterday or maybe even, if I'm letting myself dream, throw her arms around me and say how glad she is that I'm okay, but she doesn't do either of those. She just stops outside the door.

"Sorry about missing lunch." I try to say it like I'd just gotten held up in class, not like I'd had a total breakdown and thought I was dying.

"That's … fine," she says, looking down at the floor.

"I'm late for rehearsal. Can we talk later? I can pick you up after dinner."

I start to ask her what's going on, but she's already walking into the auditorium. "Yeah. Later," I say. But I'm not even sure she hears me.

————————

The house is empty when I get home. Mom and Dad are both working late. I turn on so many lights that you can probably see the house from the moon. Aliens might just land in the back yard.

The longer I wait, the more nervous I get about Ally giving me the cold shoulder.

I stand by the door like a prisoner getting ready to be taken to the gallows. Only there's this song in my head.

In 1955, a guy named Tom Lehrer recorded a song called "The Elements." Basically, he sings the names of the elements from the periodic table beginning with antimony and ending with sodium. They aren't sung in alphabetical order. Just the way that they fit best with the music.

When I was six, my dad thought it would be really funny if I learned it. I couldn't sing then either, but it didn't matter. My parents' friends thought it was hysterical to hear a little boy listing the entire periodic table when none of them could have done it themselves.

For some reason, while I'm pacing a hole in the carpet waiting for Ally to pick me up, the only thing going through my mind is that damned song.

Somewhere around "potassium, plutonium," Ally's car pulls into the drive.

Potassium is a type of salt. If you don't get enough of it, you develop all sorts of neurological problems. Plutonium blows shit up. It's all kind of fitting.

Ally doesn't get out of her car so I lock up the house and head out to meet her. I get in the passenger's side and she doesn't even look at me.

"Ally..." I start, but she cuts me off.

"No. Just. Not yet." She puts the car into gear and pulls out of the driveway. I'm dead, I think. And I totally deserve it. Why couldn't I have just kept my shit together rather than having a total freak-out in school? I stay quiet and then it becomes clear that we're heading to Central's campus. As she winds through the maze-like streets, I can see the looming outfield towers in the Warrior's outfield. She parks near the field and motions for me to get out, so I do. I'm pretty good at following orders anyhow, but my guilt and confusion are making it my only option. She could probably tell me to run laps and I would.

It's only five thirty. The campus is alive with students rushing to and from dinner and classes and who knows what else, but the field is quiet. I look at her, puzzled.

"Road game," she says in a monotone. She unlocks a side door that I wouldn't have noticed. I wonder what the hell we're doing here, but I'm relieved that if the team is playing an away game, her dad won't be here to beat the shit out of me for pissing off his daughter.

Baseball stadiums have a certain smell. Concrete, mowed

grass, sweat, hot dogs, the leather of the mitts; it all forms some sort of baseball perfume that wraps around me and for one glorious second it makes it hard for me to remember why we're really here.

Ally leads me up to the upper deck, first row behind home plate. She has no way of knowing it, but these are my favorite seats in any stadium. She sits down and I follow her lead. And then, for the first time today, she looks straight at me. Her face is tired and beautiful, and Lizzie's heart feels like it's corralled in my too-small chest.

I think about what Spencer said about moving on and living. Maybe this is the first step. Maybe this is my one chance. I'm not sure I even deserve it, but it feels like my only opportunity to find out. I take a deep breath and lean over, gripping the railing and looking over the perfectly manicured field. I don't really know where to start, but know I need to get it all out there. Every last thing. It doesn't matter if she tells everyone in the school and they all think I'm a freak. I can't stay stuck.

"Cal." Something in the nervous way she says my name forces my hand.

I take a deep breath. "I'm sorry I missed lunch yesterday. I was in the hospital. I thought I was dying, I really did." I can't even bring myself to look at her so I just talk to the field. "I've been panicking a lot lately. I guess. See, I really, really like you. I mean, I more than like you. There's never been another girl that I've liked before." I know that I'm rambling, saying things that have nothing to do with each other, but I feel like I've opened a vein and my feelings are pouring out like blood and pooling at her feet. It doesn't help that, out of everything I have to tell her, the fact that I thought I was dying is the easy stuff.

I glance at her and she's chewing on her bottom lip. I'm glad she isn't saying anything because if I don't keep talking I'm going to freak out.

"Look, you're going to think I'm crazy and maybe I am. But that's okay. I still have to tell you this. I need you to know. I can hear her. Lizzie. I can feel her inside me and sometimes I hear her voice. She talks to me, Ally."

I tell her about Lizzie's locker and how it made me feel like I was dying to watch the inside of it being painted over, and how I couldn't get Lizzie to stop wailing in my head. I have no idea if she understands why that meant I couldn't come meet her. Why it meant that I couldn't do anything besides go out to the field and beat the crap out of bats and cry. But there's more to come.

I pause, steeling myself. Ally is watching me with a blank paralyzed look on her face. I have absolutely no idea what she's thinking, which is scaring me more than it would if she were yelling or telling me she thinks I'm crazy and never wants to see me again. And somehow, I know that I have to take that blankness away and make her feel something. If I'm ever going to be able to move forward, I need to lay myself out in front of her and hope she accepts it.

"And, there's something else. Before you and I were talking, before we were at the field that first day..." Ally cocks her head and waits. "Lizzie...I..." I don't know how to say it so I force myself to say each word staccato-like, like a machine gun. "We. Kissed. Spencer. It was Lizzie. I didn't lie to you. The rumors really aren't true. This was just... I don't know. I just felt like I needed to tell you."

I finally breathe again and wait for her response. My body is humming. I feel like I've just stepped off a cliff. All I can hear is the blood racing in my ears. I wait as long as I can and then have to break the heavy silence that hangs between us.

"Ally, say something," I beg.

She looks at me and before she speaks, I know that I've ruined any chance I had with her.

"I can't do this. *Us*," she says. "I thought I could, but I can't. I mean, it isn't like I'm your girlfriend or anything, right?"

"Well, I thought... I mean, I was hoping..." I shut up because there is nothing I can say. We haven't named our relationship. I did think and hope that maybe we were becoming something, but like I've been about so many other things, I'm obviously wrong about that. I get it, though. I knew before I confessed that she might not be able to handle what happened with Spencer, but I had to come clean.

We sit there for a few minutes and then I follow her silently to her car. Neither of us says anything on the way back. She snuffles like she's trying to hold in tears. When we pull up in front of my house, I try one last time. "Ally, it will never happen again. I promise. Lizzie..."

Ally puts her hands up and stops me. "I... it doesn't matter. I'm sorry. I just can't."

She stares straight ahead until I get out of the car and stand, dazed, on the curb, watching her drive off.

TWENTY-SIX

I avoid everyone at school the next day. After the initial concern over my physical health died down yesterday, fear over my mental health kicked in and everyone is avoiding me anyhow. The one exception is Spencer, who finally tracks me down as I'm standing in front of the locker that used to be Lizzie's.

"It's not hers anymore," he says, coming up behind me.

I turn and lean my head against the cool metal. "It's like she's slipping away."

Spencer pauses before he says, "She's already gone. You just need to realize that."

My first reaction is anger. I turn around and say, "Don't we owe her more than that?"

"You owe yourself something too," he says, turning and leaning back on the locker next to me. "What happened with you and Ally?"

"There is no me and Ally." The words feel horrible coming out of my mouth. But I spent the night coming to some sort of resignation with the fact that losing Ally somehow makes karmic sense in light of what I did to Lizzie. I'm numb from all this resignation. I will, as Spencer said, live. I want to. And I'm not going to waste Lizzie's sacrifice. But for the first time, something about this loss makes sense.

Spencer turns his head and gives me a look I've only seen

him use onstage. "If you've ever trusted me about anything, trust me about this. You need to talk to her."

Behind my back, my hand finds the combination lock and squeezes hard enough to leave a mark. I didn't think it was possible to overdose on pain, but I've reached the point where I'm not sure that I can take on any more. "I told her about…" I start to say Lizzie, but even in my haze I care about Spencer too much to burden him with that. "I told her about what happened in The Cave. She bolted."

Spencer's eyes widen. I can see the flash of surprise in them, followed by disbelief. "I honestly don't think that Ally would care if you French-kissed a wombat."

I don't think there's any laughter left inside me, but this at least makes me smile.

"I've always thought of you as more of a koala," I say in a lame attempt at a joke. "It doesn't matter. This way I can't hurt her too. And I trust you, but she said she doesn't want anything to do with me."

On the other side of me, someone coughs. "I didn't say I didn't want anything to do with you. I said I couldn't."

I don't know if Ally came to find me or if it's a bad coincidence that we're all standing in the hall together.

"I'm just going to…" Spencer points down the hall. I have the urge to grab his arm and keep him here in the hope that he can make sense of what's happening. He seems to be able to read Ally better than I can. Something in his eyes tells me to fight for the future. I want to; it's just that standing against Lizzie's locker with Ally looking like she hadn't slept since yesterday makes it hard to believe that I can have a future. Or at least one where I can get close to someone without hurting them.

"Can we go outside?" Ally asks.

I follow her out to the field. Somehow Ally and I always end up on a baseball diamond. I sit on the visitor's bench but she stays standing, nervously dragging one foot through the dirt.

"I'm sorry about how I acted yesterday. I'm sorry I freaked out," she says.

"No. I get it. I do." She'd already admitted to hearing all the rumors about us. No surprise she freaked when I confirmed that at least some of them were true.

She runs a hand through her hair. "I keep thinking that I'm over it. You know? For years after Grandma died, I wouldn't even let Dad go out in the evenings. I'd just cry and cry."

"What? I don't understand."

She puts her arms around herself and says, "When we started working with the team, you were running and everything. I mean, I knew what you'd been through. But you seemed fine. And then when you didn't show up for lunch the other day, I went to look for you. And all I heard was that you'd been taken to the hospital. That it was your heart. Justin even told me that he heard you'd died."

She looks like she might cry and that's the only thing that keeps me from finding Justin Dillard and killing him.

"But I'm fine. I *am* fine. Ally, what's this about?" I take her hand and pull her back down to the bench next to me.

"I can't stand to lose one more person," she says in an

eerie echo of my own thoughts. "I'm seventeen. I can't spend every day worrying that my boyfriend is going to die."

Boyfriend? "I thought you said we weren't..." I stop mid-sentence because suddenly the word "die" rings even louder in my ears. "I'm not dying, Ally. I might be a panicky freak with his best friend's heart. But I'm not going anywhere."

To prove my point I fall on the ground and do ten push-ups. Then I race to the pitcher's mound and back. When I pick her up and start spinning around, she actually starts to laugh.

She links her arms around my neck. Somewhere in my head I hear *Live, Live, Live* only I'm not sure if it's Lizzie's voice or my own or even Spencer's.

"You can't promise me that," she whispers with the same lost expression she had on her face when she was over at my house and told me about her mom and her grandmother and her aunt, and it all becomes clear.

I put her down so that she's standing on home plate, my heart racing and my head a jumble of sound. "No, I can't promise. No one can. But I don't think I'm dying faster than anyone else." If I'm surprised by my own words, I hope it doesn't show.

"I'm sorry that I'm scared," she says.

"I'm sorry that I am too," I admit. "Not about being sick, just... I don't want to lose you."

She squeezes my hand and doesn't let go. "Maybe we can just slow down and see how it goes, together?"

I take a deep breath and enjoy the strong beat of Lizzie's heart. "So you aren't freaked out by the fact that I'm responsible for what happened to Lizzie?"

"You're a bonehead, Ryan. Seriously," she says and it puzzles me because despite the words she's using, her voice is soft and sweet. "Spencer told me how you spent your entire life making sure that Lizzie stayed safe. How you never let yourself not be there for her. Man, you wouldn't even talk to me because of it."

"That's not…" I start, but she puts a finger to my lips and I shut up. I can feel her breath on my face and it sends shivers up my back.

"You didn't kill her, Cal. You're fighting like hell to keep her alive inside you."

Is that what this is? Could it really be so simple? Before I ask Ally, she answers my questions.

"I don't think you're crazy. I think it must be wonderful to hear her voice and feel her with you. It must make missing her a hell of a lot easier."

I sink like a perfectly thrown pitch and Ally kneels down next to me. How it is possible that she's managed to make sense of everything when I couldn't? When not even Spencer or Dr. Reynolds could?

"But you need to let her go just a little because I don't think I want to walk away from this… from you… without a fight. I'm already fighting myself. I don't want to fight Lizzie too." Ally smiles. "She could probably wipe the floor with me. There has to be room for both of us in there."

She puts her hand, palm flat, onto my chest. I can feel Lizzie's heart beating against it.

Without thinking I start to lean in to kiss her and then pull back. "Wait. So does that mean you aren't upset about me and Spencer either?"

Her face is unreadable and for a minute I think that I should have kept my mouth shut. Maybe she'd even forgotten what I told her. But I see a little smile play across the corners of her mouth.

"Nah, that's actually kinda hot." I know that I'm standing there with my mouth open like an idiot. "But it's just us from now on, right?"

I nod again. I wonder if I'm ever going to be able to get to the point where she doesn't surprise me at every turn. I wonder if I'd ever want to.

TWENTY-SEVEN

I drive the safe, reliable, boring-as-crap Volvo my parents got me to my next meeting with Dr. Reynolds. I'm still shaky behind the wheel, but he was right when he said that driving would get easier every time. And since I'm driving and he seems to think I'm getting a grip on things, I'm not going to meet with him for a few weeks and see how that goes.

But this time I share my list. Not the one about Ally, which now runs onto multiple pages, because that one is just for me, but the list about Lizzie.

I don't really have anything written down to show him but, for the first time, I'm able to talk about it and once I start, just like driving, it gets easier.

Dr. Reynolds listens and doesn't tell me I'm crazy either. In fact, he says he thinks that my hearing her voice and feeling like she's with me makes sense. His theory is that since she was such a big part of my life, it's to be expected, given everything, given that I have part of her inside me, that my brain would try to find a way to keep her with me. He says that so long as she isn't telling me to jump off of bridges or anything that he isn't worried.

He tells me that Ally sounds wonderful and I agree. We talk a little about Ally's issues. And we decide that I'm going to ask her to come with me the next time I go to see Dr. Collins so that he can explain my prognosis to her.

I talk about how Ally and I have been hanging out with Spencer some and it's strange. I mean, there was a certain dynamic with me, Lizzie, and Spencer that I'd been used to for so long. And this is completely different. Not bad— there is definitely nothing bad about it—but it's strangely easy. It's like Spencer and I were always trying to keep the teeter-totter that was Lizzie perfectly level. It was a lot of work, and both of us were always trying to make sure things didn't tip too far in one direction or another, that she didn't fall off and take us down with her. With Ally, it's like everything is just even to begin with. We can let our guards down and know that everything will be okay.

I thought I'd crossed Reynolds' last hurdle with the list thing, but no. There's one more thing he wants me to do and it won't be easy. In fact, it might be the hardest thing I've ever done, including telling Ally about what happened in The Cave that night.

I tell him that I'll think about it, but really, I'm not ready to go to the cemetery yet. In fact, I don't know that I'll ever be ready, even though Spencer and Ally have made it clear that they agree with Dr. Reynolds in thinking it might help. Even though they're going tomorrow. Even though they want me to come with them.

The whole next day in school I try to think about something else, baseball or Ally, but Lizzie's laughter fills the hallway and I hear, *Not my combination, Cal. I don't even have a locker anymore.*

I pull on the lock and realize that I've been trying to open my locker with Lizzie's combination. This is, I guess, my new normal and I'd better get used to it. Maybe I'll just change my numbers to hers. It would make things easier.

I enter the right combination just as I hear "oof" behind me and something slides into my foot. I glance down and then turn and gloat at Justin Dillard hobbling down the hall on a broken ankle and now missing a crutch, which is lying on the floor in front of me. I'd almost feel bad for him had he broken the bone in a game or something, but rumor has it that he broke it falling over a curb in the parking lot while he was hitting on a freshman, so I'm not going to get worked up about it.

I lift my foot and put it down lightly on the crutch.

"Come on, Ryan. Don't be a dick." Justin's eyes are pleading for me to stop.

"Seriously? You going to insult me? You must not want this back in one piece."

He hops on his good foot and winces. "Sorry. Can you just give that back?"

We've got a couple of minutes before class and part of me wants to drag this out as long as possible. It's nice to see him look contrite. For once.

"Did you know you have a huge splinter on your foot?" Spencer moves up next to me and I'm even more amused by the fact that he's playing along than I am at giving Dillard a hard time.

Justin narrows his eyes and looks back and forth between us and I wait for him to say whatever horrible thing is on his mind, but then he literally bites his lip and I have to laugh.

I bend down to pick up the crutch and slide it across the floor. "Get out of here," I say and start to stand, but something catches my eye. There in the bottom corner of my locker is a tiny painting of a cow wearing a Detroit Tigers' cap jumping over a moon surrounded by a couple of surprisingly accurate constellations. The whole thing is about the size of a silver dollar. I could have easily gone the whole year without seeing it.

I sit down and examine each perfect brush stroke and the tiny initials underneath: *LM*.

Spencer kneels next to me to see what I'm staring at. "She started it," he says in a voice filled with awe.

I promised.

I grab my phone and do what I should have done with her locker: I take a photo. I'm not losing this message from her.

"Thanks, Lizzie." I whisper it even though the hallway is loud with students and only Spencer is close enough to hear. "Thank you."

I'm determined not to cry and wish I could find some way to thank her that's more public than talking to her in my head.

Spencer watches me, waiting to see how I'm going to react. He's ready to pick up the pieces as usual. But this time I'm not going to fall apart. This time I just want to do the right thing to honor the friend that I love and miss so much.

"I'll do it," I say to him in a broken voice. "I'll go with you."

And that's how I find myself after school in a new blue suit on a beautiful spring day, in the back of Spencer's car. I'm shivering like it's suddenly winter, and Ally keeps reaching through the space between the seats to hold my hand. I think she's as freaked out as I am, but there's no doubt in my mind that it's only their voices and the flow of the periodic table through my head keeping me together.

I keep my eyes closed through the whole drive and it's only when I realize they've stopped talking and the car has stopped moving that I open them.

I never thought I could ever go to a cemetery, yet here I am. Rows and rows of gray headstones stand at attention like concrete soldiers. Some have flags. Some have flowers. Some have nothing and these last ones make my chest constrict.

I sit in the car, paralyzed like I've forgotten how to open a car door. Spencer and Ally exchange looks like protective parents before getting out of the car and coming around to my door.

I take each of their hands in one of mine, and they pull me out, and we begin walking.

My suit is itchy and hot. I had a black one that used to get dragged out for athletic department dinners, but it didn't fit anymore. This new blue one already feels tainted. I don't want something that I only wear to cemeteries.

As we walk, Ally and Spencer keep hold of my hands, which is good because I'm watching the sky rather than my feet. Puffy cumulous clouds are dotted around like cotton balls and I focus on them until we stop and I'm forced to look at what's in front of us.

The headstone is gray marble like the others. For a minute I'm relieved because I think that we're in the wrong place since the grave is labeled, "Elizabeth Marie McDonald" and I don't remember Lizzie ever going by anything other than Lizzie or Liz. But then I feel my heart miss a beat and I know that this really *is* her grave.

Ally tightens her grip on my hand while Spencer bends down and places a bouquet of wild flowers onto the soil.

Some flowers are already scattered over the grave. Some are planted—I guess my mom and Spencer's have been busy—but there are a few scattered on the grass as well: fading, dried red roses next to some that look like they were just delivered by a florist. I know Lizzie didn't really have any friends beside us; Spencer must come here more than I know.

We stand there for a few minutes. I'm not sure what we're supposed to do so I start counting a bunch of rocks that are placed haphazardly on top of the marble.

"What's with the stones?" I quietly ask no one in particular.

Spencer picks a small round rock off the ground and adds it to the pile. "It's for respect," he answers. "So that the person knows they've had visitors."

That seems odd. I mean, everyone here is dead; they aren't out running errands. Spencer's explanation makes the stones sound like some type of cosmic voicemail.

Spencer opens up a bag I didn't realize he had and pulls out one of those LED candles he had in The Cave.

"The cemetery won't let you bring in real candles because of all the grass." He turns it on and puts that on top of the headstone as well. I think back to what he said about ghost lights and about how they're meant to keep the good, creative spirits around. Lizzie would like that.

Actually, as I look around, I think that Spencer was right when he said that she'd like this whole place. There's a pond and all sorts of bushes that are in bloom. I think if she were here, she'd already have climbed to the top of the tall tree that's casting shadows all around us. She'd be lobbing acorns at my head. That idea makes me smile, which isn't what I was expecting to do here.

Spencer grabs my arm and gives a little tug, then points to a grave a few rows away. "Do you see that?"

I squint. That grave has a candle on it too.

"Alice Tylor," he says. "The girl who killed herself in The Cave. A bunch of us decided to take turns making sure it stays lit, at least until graduation anyhow."

Ally's arm wraps around my waist and it feels like it belongs there. It's getting hard to imagine there was ever a time when all I could do was watch her across hallways.

"Can you guys do something for me?" Spencer asks.

He takes a deep breath and looks from one to the other of us and I know whatever he's asking means something to him; something important.

"My dad is speaking at a conference in Seattle. He…my parents bought me a ticket to go too," he says with a half-smile directed right at me. "They think I need to spend some time with Rob in person." If he weren't smiling, I'd think they'd had a fight or something, but Spencer doesn't look upset. In fact, he's pretty much glowing. "I guess I've learned that you can't take time for granted." He shrugs, looking slightly embarrassed and a little young. "It's time to take my own advice."

"Wow. Cool parents," Ally says. I have to remind myself that she doesn't know Spencer well, so she wouldn't know that all his parents said when he came out to them was, "We know." Just like with us, it just didn't really matter. I suspect that they've been giving him as hard a time about seeing Rob as Spencer gave me about talking to Ally.

Here in the quiet of the cemetery, with Spencer on one side, Ally on the other, and Lizzie seemingly everywhere, I find myself in the middle of a memory of first grade.

I honestly don't remember a time before I knew Spencer. We met in preschool or maybe even before. But in first grade, we met Lizzie. She was tiny, with long dark hair and a haunted sad look to her eyes. She walked into the first day of class late and Spencer and I looked at her and then at each other. Somehow we both knew she'd be important to us.

At recess, instead of joining the other girls, she stood against a wall and watched everyone. She looked so deep in thought that I never would have said anything. But Spencer recognized something in her, I guess. When he told her to eat lunch with us, her whole face lit up and she gave him a smile that seemed to seal our futures.

I look at Spencer now, watching him smile at Ally—it's a different smile from what he offered to Lizzie, but it gives me a similar feeling of completion.

"Yeah," he says with a glint in his eye. "My parents are great. I was just wondering if you could take care of the ghost lights. Just while I'm gone."

Ally doesn't let go of my hand, but she leans over me and pulls Spencer into a hug. "Of course we will," she says, looking at me for confirmation.

I nod.

The wind picks up a little and I hear the tree leaves rustle in it. And that's when I realize that the wind is all I'm hearing. I search my brain for Lizzie's voice, for some sound, but for the first time since the hospital I don't hear anything at all. Not even the sound of her blood coursing through me.

This silence is odd and makes me feel lonely. I'd gotten used to Lizzie being in my head even though it freaked me out.

But then I think that maybe this is how it's meant to be. Maybe we each need to be alone at some point so that we can consciously choose who we want in our lives, who we want to be a part of us.

I stand there watching Spencer. I know, without even having to think about it, that I can count on him for anything. And then I look at Ally and I have to smile because she didn't know Lizzie and yet she's here. Just for me. Just to help. So even though Lizzie's voice is gone from my head, I'm not alone. I realize that now. And really, I don't think that Lizzie will ever totally be gone so long as I have her heart inside me.

But I guess what remains after someone you love dies aren't things you can reach out and touch. When you love someone, that love changes you for better or worse. So in a way, maybe they're never truly gone.

I kneel down and touch the dirt on Lizzie's grave. I expect it to feel different, but instead it feels surprisingly like the dirt on a baseball infield.

"I'm sorry," I whisper for the last time. "I'll never forget you. Ever. You'll always be a part of me."

As I stand up and brush the dirt off my pant legs, the breeze kicks up again. I get a whiff of some sort of flowers and then it starts raining with them. Ally, Spencer, and I hold hands as white and pink flower petals float over us like snow. Somewhere, I think, Lizzie is smiling.

People throw around phrases without thinking all the time. They say they're having a change of heart when they're really just changing their minds. I mean, there are only around 2,200 transplants done in the US each year, so there aren't a lot of people who know what it really feels like to change your heart.

Then there are people who say that they've learned something "by heart." But really they've just used their brain to memorize it.

And I know for a fact that you can't really steal someone's heart. You can't just break them in two and take it. They have to open up their chest and give it to you willingly.

A few of the phrases make more sense to me. Absence can really make the heart grow fonder, but I think it's better to show how much you like someone while they're still around. I think Spencer has finally clued in to that.

And we all know how you can carelessly break someone's heart.

Some people really do seem to wear their heart on their sleeve. I guess I fall into that category.

I watch Ally and Spencer standing together under the rain of flower petals, and Lizzie's heart—mine now—feels so full that I don't know how my body can contain it.

It won't always be easy and that's okay. Maybe everyone learns this lesson in a different way, maybe all friendships need to be tested and changed so you know that they still mean something.

I lean down and pick up a smooth stone and lay it on Lizzie's headstone and smile. Whoever said "follow your heart" got it right.

Acknowledgments

Writing might be a solitary pursuit, but publishing takes a village. To Dana Allison Levy, Stephanie Cardel, and Carmen Erickson, who were always there to add their voices to the village of *What Remains*, THANK YOU, and LOVE, and ALL GOOD THINGS.

Immense thanks, also, to:

Levi Buchanan, Leah O'Brien Bernini, Cara West Aston, Suzanne Kamata, and Chris Tower, for reading and answering all of my crazy writer questions.

Robert L. Galloway Jr., PhD, for making sure my medical questions got to the people who could answer them.

Charlotte Rains Dixon, for the best five minutes of brainstorming imaginable. I owe you.

Beth Hull and AdriAnne Strickland, for stepping in at the thirteenth hour to save me from tripping over my own feet.

Tessa Gratton, who gave a wanna-be author just the right amount of encouragement and advice to see it through. I hope that someday I can inspire someone the way you inspired me.

The illustrious Andrew Smith and Matthew MacNish, for putting me through query letter boot camp and rewarding me with some amazing bourbon recommendations when I finally got it right.

The entire crew of SCBWI-MidSouth, particularly Courtney Stevens, David Arnold, Kristin Tubb, Rae Ann Parker, Alisha Klapheke, Ashley Schwartau, and Ashley Blake. You guys manage to make the business of publishing feel like the warmth of community. And to Parnassus Books and Stephanie Appell, for always supporting local writers.

Melissa Jeglinski, for finding a seed of this book in Authoress's Baker's Dozen contest and allowing it to make her cry in her office, and Beth Phelan, for being a sane voice in a crazy industry.

My editor, Brian Farrey-Latz, for a great debate and a wombat that was just too good to discard, and to Sandy Sullivan, Mallory Hayes, and the gang at Flux, particularly the art department who made my dreams come true and then turned around and did it again.

To Joe, who believed in ghosts and who haunts the Cave scenes of this book. I suspect you lurk somewhere in the Dungeon waiting for unsuspecting theater majors to lure you out.

Also, as *What Remains* is ultimately a love story of friendship, I'd be remiss not to mention my Kalamazoo College friends to whom this book is dedicated, as well as my father, Harold Baker, and his amazing "brothers," Don David and Ed Kohl. You prove, every day, that friends are what make the world go round.

And to John and Keira, with love.

About the Author

Helene Dunbar is the author of *These Gentle Wounds* (Flux, 2014) and *What Remains* (Flux, 2015). Over the years, she's worked as a drama critic, journalist, and marketing manager, and has written on topics as diverse as Irish music, court cases, theater, and Native American tribes. She lives in Nashville with her husband and daughter, and exists on a steady diet of readers' tears.